P9-DTO-052

The Gold Diggers

FOR
MY FATHER

XMAS
1974

BARRY

By Robert Creeley

PIECES
WORDS
THE GOLD DIGGERS
THE ISLAND
FOR LOVE

A QUICK GRAPH
THE CHARM

The
Gold Diggers

AND OTHER STORIES

by

ROBERT CREELEY

Charles Scribner's Sons NEW YORK

Copyright © 1965 Robert Creeley
Copyright 1951, 1953, © 1955, 1961 Robert Creeley.

Some of these stories were first published in the following magazines:
Evergreen Review, Kenyon Review, New Directions Annual 13, New Mexico Quarterly, Origin and *Poetry, Taos.*

A shorter version of this book was published in a limited edition by the Divers Press, Mallorca, in 1954.

This book published simultaneously in the
United States of America and in Canada —
Copyright under the Berne Convention.

All rights reserved. No part of this book
may be reproduced in any form without the
permission of Charles Scribner's Sons.

A — 1.72[M]

Printed in the United States of America
Library of Congress Catalog Card Number 65-23982
SBN 684-12724-5 (trade paper, SL)

Contents

For my Mother

Preface

Had I lived some years ago, I think I would have been a moralist, i.e., one who lays down, so to speak, rules of behavior with no small amount of self-satisfaction. But the writer isn't allowed that function anymore, or no man can take the job on very happily, being aware (as he must be) of what precisely that will make him.

So there is left this other area, still the short story or really the tale, and all that can be made of it. Whereas the novel is a continuum, of necessity, chapter to chapter, the story can escape some of that obligation, and function exactly in terms of whatever emotion best can serve it.

The story has no time finally. Or it hasn't here. Its shape, if form can be so thought of, is a sphere, an egg of obdurate kind. The only possible reason for its existence is that it has, in itself, the fact of reality and the pressure. There, in short, is its form—no matter how random and broken that will seem. The old assumptions of beginning and end—those very neat assertions—have fallen way completely in a place where the only actuality is life, the only end (never realised) death, and the only value, what love one can manage.

It is impossible to think otherwise, or at least I have found it so. I begin where I can, and end when I see the whole thing returning. Perhaps that is an obsession. These people, and what happens to them here, have never been completely my decision—because if you once say something, it will lead you to say more than you had meant to.

As the man responsible, I wanted to say what I thought was true, and make that the fact. It has led me to impossible things at times. I was not obliged, certainly, to say anything, but that argument never made sense to me.

R. C.

The Unsuccessful Husband

•

The
Unsuccessful Husband

Such a day of peace it was, so calm and quiet, with the
haze at the window, beginning, and from there going far
out over the fields to the river beyond, a morning haze, such
as the sun soon burns and has done with. Yet all through that
day there was quiet and the haze of calm. It was not the
first of many such days. None followed. But it became the
reminder of something somewhat better than what one had,
the stasis of peace, which, once found, can always remind
one and even be found again. Such a day, a peaceful day, so
calm and quiet, one is never done with, no matter how
long . . .

We were married fifteen years ago at a quiet ceremony
attended by a very few people, close friends, and following
the ceremony we travelled to a place where I had not been
since my childhood but where, as it were, I had always
lived or at least wanted to. My wife was then a very pretty
woman, a quiet face with a smile of destructive calm, and a
figure which, at the very least, provoked one to thoughts
not quite in keeping with a usual intention. I cannot say
how it was but it was simply that she could not be won, not
in the usual manner. Although I do not remember it as

11

deliberate, still I can see now that it was a matter of giving in the old sense such as I had believed no longer to exist. Nothing so much suggested it as when, after we had eaten and had spent what was left of the evening reading, perhaps, with some time of quiet conversation, she would at last turn to me with an air of permission and would then rise and set about the task of going to bed. What I had expected was not necessarily something more, but certainly something different, and when on that first night I was so permitted, I saw that nothing again would ever be as I intended it, never what I had hoped for.

I am not a successful man in any sense of the word and if my wife has permitted me in her own way, the rest of the world has allowed me to live in another. I have never been openly molested, not with intention of the sort I might imagine for myself. I have often thought that an open attack might be fairer for all concerned but I can see now that I was only thinking of myself. Others seemed not to care that much and I suppose that they had every right not to. I have annoyed them but, after all, I have never essentially disturbed their lives. Let live, they say, and they know what they are doing.

The fact of my failure can be seen in many instances but it is not so much this fact as the other of my not having been a success. Because, after all, I haven't failed if it was my own intention not to be successful, although to anyone else it would seem so. I will allow that I am not successful but I confess it is more difficult to admit of my failure. I agree to the compromise but must reserve the choice for myself.

When it was that I first gave evidence of my intention to be an unsuccessful man, I do not remember. In any event it was a long time ago and quite probably not long after our marriage. Before that time I was not quite so sure as I am now of the fact that it is at all costs necessary to oppose oneself to the determinations of one's destroyers. I had not then thought that my wife would be in some sense their general. But it turned out so and soon after I began the task of opposition on whatever level they should choose. Though I have never been successful, even in this, I have the eventual satisfaction of a life so empty that even they will be hard put to it for praises.

At the time of our marriage my wife had a small sum of money with which we intended to make our start. This sum she put at my disposal, to use in whatever way I thought best. She had given me this sum or rather she had given me a check on her bank for the amount and told me that it was now mine to do with as I pleased. So, taking the check, I set out toward the business district of the town and when I had come to the first bank, I went in and deposited the check in her name. And there it has been ever since.

This gesture, which was, to be sure, very much a gesture, began the understanding between my wife and myself which was never obscured in all our years of living together, which did, in fact, survive those years more gracefully than we ourselves. It was an altogether simple act, half-understood and at best angry, but it served us better than any of the more deliberate ones that followed. Nothing made it quite so plain to each of us where the other stood and there never was a better reminder.

I would often say to my wife who was not so well controlled that she could forbear mention of the money at all times, that when I had at last made my fortune, this money we would use to make a wonderful time for ourselves,

spending it on a trip to the Bahamas or some such nonsensi-
cal place. On such occasions she would smile and laugh a
little but the success of my wit had really more to do with
the fact of my certainty that even should I have had those
tickets in my hand at that very moment, she would have
laughed just as delightfully and would not have moved one
inch from her chair. The surety with which we grew to deal
with one another was actually what delighted us and we
always knew exactly what to say. If it had not been for the
money to begin with, it would not have been so easy and
this first gesture of mine served as model for many more.
Still, if my gesture seemed the first, and the money the
source of all our understanding, as time passed I began to
understand my wife a little more acutely than at first and
also to see that if it was I who had put the money to such
good use, it was, nevertheless, she who had had the good
sense to give it to me.

In past years I have often had called to my attention the
constant infidelities of husbands and wives which marked
them much more than they would have, had they been
confined to the flesh only. Because flesh is at best flesh and
would look as poor as any hanging in a butcher's window.
But these whom I have watched were dealing primarily
with other values, with lives in a more total sense, and they
could only be condemned for their lack of understanding.
Their bickering was constant, never-ending, and the wives
waited only for the moment when their husbands would
return from their various jobs so that it could all begin
again. And I suspect that even the husbands hurried a little
faster on their way home from work, to get at it and to miss
as little as they possibly could. For myself, perhaps a month
or two would pass before either my wife or myself was

aware of our differences. Perhaps they were not even differences but rather our unholy similarities, our understandings. We were not thought to be unhappy, to be fighting all of the time, and to tell the truth we weren't. But I suspect that each of us was sure that there was, after all something better though we had long since given up trying to think about it. It was the suggestion of this which reminded us, which gave us all our pleasure.

Yet we did live together in a way which few people do nowadays. We dealt with one another constantly and were never put off, never refused unless it were a condition of our understanding that was in question. We knew one another as well as anyone ever knew another and, if it had not been for our loathing, we should have been happy.

Other people, although I don't for a moment believe that what they say is true, at least claim a continuity in their lives, a going up or a coming down. The rise or fall which they maintain is their way of saying that they have lived and even those who stay in the middle suppose that they narrowly missed worse or very nearly achieved better. For me this does not apply, and I find it very hard to believe that it does even for others. If I say that I got to know my wife better during the time we lived together, what I intend to say is that after a time I knew her whereas before that time she was no better for my uses than an utter stranger. Neither of us lived for much more than ourselves, one another, though not in the usual sense. God knows we lived long enough, both of us, though I can't say we grew older or younger or that we grew at all. If one lives at all, one lives for the kind of things that my wife and I lived for, understandings, the security of knowledge. One certainly does not live to grow old.

But now for my purposes it is necessary to suppose a continuity although none comes readily to hand. What my wife said a year ago is no more to the point than what she said on our wedding night. There is nothing to suggest that we have lived in between. No, for both of us, it was like going past some beautiful spot, stopping to look, and then never leaving, always looking to see more and more and more. We never tired of one another and we spent our lives in such looking though at times we might wish to be gone. But still we stayed where we were.

Taken only as years our life seems very uneventful. After our marriage we settled in the town where we spent the days of our honeymoon, an acquiescence on the part of my wife which I was then still too confused to understand. Now I see that it was for her purposes, not mine, that we settled there for it was intended that I should fail on home-ground, so to speak. It was to be the place of my failure or at least the place of my giving proof. But my failure was never what they intended or, because they so deliberately intended it, it was not really mine. I was an unsuccessful man to be sure, but the failure was all theirs. Had they intended my success, it would have been something else again but, as it was, the failure belonged to them.

I can remember the occasions of the first trials quite well just as I can remember almost all of my relations with my wife. A friend would sponsor me, set me up in business, and then quite quietly I would fail. It was always the same, always followed by the half-expressed reproaches from the friend. They could never say that I did not try because I did but what they forgot was my own intelligence which made each of my efforts consistently contributive to my ruin. It was a way I had about which they really knew nothing. My wife knew though, perhaps, not as well as I, but it was for her own purposes that she never said anything and always expressed her confidence in me with the same sure tone, just as if nothing had happened. If at first I was tempted to tell her why I so often failed, I soon saw that she knew quite well without my telling and it was better for all concerned to keep silent.

Such conduct on my part was never very simple and I always envied my wife her own part. She was never obliged to come and go as I was, never forced into tedious misrepresentations, never compelled to show failure if not actually to fail. On some evenings I came home as tired as any honest man, no matter what I had been up to, but never was there anything more than what I had left in the morning. Gently my wife would question me about the day's work and I would answer that it had gone well and that I was sure that soon everything would be all right. It was our particular joke, this question and answer and it never failed to bring a smile from my wife. But it was never quite so simple for me because there were those evenings when I wished that my own work had gone for something more than jokes whose humor was not always so apparent.

It was wrong of me to worry and I did worry quite often during the middle of our life together. At that time it became more difficult than I had thought possible for me to keep my own attitude free of the suggestion of failure directed at me from every side. My wife's friends came frequently to call during that time, and when I came in from work I found them there with my wife, waiting no less than she to see how my day had gone. Perhaps my wife agreed after awhile to the more private engagement I had intended because after some time had passed, her friends were no longer there when I came in and once again it was only my wife I had to face. To me this seemed fairer and moreover it was she whom they had chosen.

It was wrong of me to worry because, as we went on, I began to see that I had very nearly won, at least so far as my wife was concerned. Perhaps it was that her questions concerning the businesses I so carefully guided into failure seemed more genuine, more tired. My own answers were never more cheerful, more full of hope, and I told her each day that perhaps tomorrow would see the final victory and, I would add with a smile, the long-promised trip to the Bahamas. I don't know if it was wrong to take advantage of her growing weakness but I was sure that if it had been I who had been first to give in, she would have been no less kind. There was little chance to do more than I had always done, those things upon which we had so long ago agreed, and I am even inclined to think that my wife would never have respected a response to her own weakness. And I wonder even now if her weakness, so persuasive in its own way, was not, after all, just another trick.

In any event the time after that was a great deal easier for me because I could begin to relax though not too much at first. I had lived with my wife too long not to realize the infinite resources at her disposal and I could suspect with some justice that at any time, a time when I should least suspect it, she would again attack and my long-built defences would fall in ruins. In consequence, I was careful, very careful, at first and then I did relax a little but she gave no sign that she noticed it, my relaxing, until at last I was almost sure that what I did no longer concerned her and my time of trial was at an end.   •

One evening I came home as usual with much the same

news and, when I came into the house, I called to her but she did not answer. It did not surprise me very much because she had begun to show signs of deafness and, although I was not altogether convinced that it was not her last attempt to defeat me, it did seem that she could not hear as well as she once had. Calling again, I went into the room where she spent most of her time and there she was, sitting in her chair. But I could see immediately from the slack position of her hands, fallen beyond the arms of her chair, that she was not well and then, when I came closer, I saw that she was dead.

The next day I have already spoken of, such a calm and peaceful day, and I spent the greater part of it arranging for her funeral. Needless to say, I had only to express a few brief wishes and the rest of the matter was taken out of my hands. The day of her funeral passed without event and I found myself watching her go into the ground without much feeling of any kind. I knew that her part in it was over and my own very nearly so. In any event it was something to think about.

•

Mr Blue

❖ Mr
❖ Blue

𝙸 don't want to give you only the grotesqueness, not only
what it then seemed. It is useless enough to remember
but to remember only what is unpleasant seems particularly
foolish. I suspect that you have troubles of your own, and,
since you have, why bother you with more. Mine against
yours. That seems a waste of time. But perhaps mine are also
yours. And if that's so, you'll find me a sympathetic listener.

A few nights ago I wrote down some of this, thinking,
trying to think, of what had happened. What had really
happened like they say. It seemed, then, that some such
effort might get me closer to an understanding of the thing
than I was. So much that was not directly related had got
in and I thought a little noting of what was basic to the
problem might be in order. That is, I wanted to analyze it,
to try to see where things stood. I'm not at all sure that it
got to anything, this attempt, because I'm not very good at
it. But you can look for yourselves.

(1) That dwarfs, gnomes, midgets are, by the fact of their
SIZE, intense;

(2) that dwarfs, gnomes, midgets cause people LARGER

23

than themselves to appear wispy, insubstantial, cardboard;

(3) that all SIZE tends towards BIG but in the case of
dwarfs, gnomes, midgets.

But perhaps best to begin at the beginning. And, to begin, there are two things that you must know. The first of
these is that I am, myself, a tall man, somewhat muscular
though not unpleasantly so. I have brown hair and brown
eyes though that is not altogether to the point here. What
you should remember is that I am a big man, as it happens,
one of the biggest in the town.

My wife is also large. This is the second. But she is not so
much large as large-boned. A big frame. I sound as though
I were selling her, but I'm not. I mean, I don't want to
sound like that, as though I were trying to impress you that
way. It is just that that I don't want to do. That is, make
you think that I am defending her or whatever it is that I
may sound like to you. In short, she is an attractive woman
and I don't think I am the only one who would find her so.
She has, like myself, brown hair but it is softer, very soft,
and she wears it long, almost to her waist, in heavy braids.
But it is like her eyes, I mean, there is that lightness in it,
the way it brushes against her back when she is walking. It
makes me feel rather blundering, heavy, to look at her. It
seems to me my step jars the house when I walk through a
room where she is. We have been married five years.

Five years doesn't seem, in itself, a very long time. So
much goes so quickly, so many things that I can think of
now that then, when they were happening, I could hardly
take hold of. And where she comes into it, those things that

had to do with her, I find I missed, perhaps, a lot that I
should have held to. At least I should have tried. But like it
or not, it's done with. Little good to think of it now.

I did try, though, to do what I could. She never seemed
unhappy, and doesn't even now. Perhaps upset when the
baby was sick, but, generally speaking, she's a level woman,
calm, good-sense.

But perhaps that's where I'm wrong, that I have that
assumption, that I think I know what she is like. Strange
that a man shouldn't know his wife but I suppose it could
be so, that even having her around him for five years, short
as they are, he could still be strange to her and she to him.
I think I know, I think I know about what she'd do if this
or that happened, if I were to say this to her, or something
about something, or what people usually talk about. It's not
pleasant doubting your own knowing, since that seems all
you have. If you lose that, or take it as somehow wrong, the
whole thing goes to pieces. Not much use trying to hold it
together after that.

Still I can't take seriously what's happened. I can't but
still I do. I wish it were different, that in some way, I were
out of it, shaken but at least out. But here I am. The same
place.

It was raining, a bad night for anything. Not hard, but
enough to soak you if you were out in it for very long. We
thought it would probably be closed but when we got
there, all the lights were going and I could see some people
up in the ferris-wheel, probably wet to the skin. Still they
looked as if they were having fun and some of their shouts
reached us as we went through the gate and into the main
grounds. It was fairly late, about ten or so, another reason

why I had thought it would be closed. Another day and the whole works would be gone and that's why she had insisted.

I feel, usually, uncomfortable in such places. I don't like the crowds, at least not the noise of them. They never seem to stop, always jumping, moving, and the noise. Any one of them, alone, or two or three, that's fine. As it happened, we went by a number of our friends, who yelled at us, fine night, or some such thing. I can't remember exactly what the words were. But I didn't like them, or didn't like them then, with that around them, the noise, and their excitement.

No reason, perhaps, to think she knew where she was going. I didn't. I think we followed only the general movement of the people, where they were going. It was packed and very difficult to go anywhere but where you were pushed. So we were landed in front of the tent without much choice and stood, listening to the barker, to see what might be happening.

I can say, and this is part of it, that I didn't want to go in. For several reasons. The main one is that I don't like freaks, I don't like to look at them or to be near them. They seem to have a particular feeling around them, which is against me, altogether. A good many times I've seen others staring, without the slightest embarrassment, at some hunchback, or some man with a deformity that puts him apart from the rest. I don't see how they can do it, how they can look without any reaction but curiosity. For myself, I want only to get away.

But this time she decided. It seemed that not very much could be inside the tent. They had advertised a midget, a knife-thrower, a man with some snakes, and one or two

other things. Nothing like the large circuses and none of the
more horrible things such might offer. So I got the tickets
and we followed a few of the others in.

They were just finishing a performance. It was so packed
at the front, that we stood at the back, waiting until the
first crowd was ready to leave. I felt tired myself. It must
have been close to eleven at that point. It seemed an effort
there was no reason for. But she enjoyed it, looked all
around, at everyone, smiled at those she knew, waved to
some, kept talking to me, and I would say something or
other to hide my own feeling. Perhaps I should have been
straight with her, told her I was tired, and ducked out. It
would have saved it, or at least got me free. But I kept
standing there, with her, waiting for the show to finish and
another to start.

It did soon, the first crowd moving out, and our own
coming up to take its place. The man on the platform had
got down at the end and now we waited for him to come
back and the new show to begin. There was talking around
us, sounding a little nervous the way most will at those
times when something is being waited for, though what one
can't say with exactness. At this point, I was almost as
expectant as the others. Nothing else to be, perhaps. In any
event, I had got over my other feeling.

The first act was a cowboy with a lariat, rope tricks. Not
much but he was good with it, could make it spin all kinds
of loops, shrinking them, making them grow right while we
watched him. It was good fun, I thought, not much but
enough. At the end he started stamping with one foot and
at the same time, he slipped his loop off and on it, brought
it up around both feet at the end, jumping and grinning. I
think there may have been some music with it, something

for the beat, but it doesn't matter. The man told us he was deaf, couldn't hear a thing. There didn't seem to be much point in telling us that but I guess we're apt to like that adding of what we don't expect.

We enjoyed it, the both of us. It's not often that we can get out, like that, to see anything. And after the first I forgot about being tired and liked it as much as she did. The next act was the knife-thrower. He could put them all in a circle no bigger than my hand, eight of them, so that they shivered there with a force which surprised me, and each time one hit, she gripped my arm, and I laughed at her nervousness, but it was a funny thing, even so.

Then came the snake act, which wasn't up to the others, or simply that dullness in it, the snakes much the same, doped, I expect, though perhaps I was wrong to think so. Then sort of a juggling act, a man with a number of colored balls and odd-shaped sticks, which he set into a strange kind of movement, tossing them, one after the other, until he must have had ten, somehow, going and all this with an intentness that made us almost clap then, as they did move, through his hands. Altogether a wonder it seemed, his precision, and how it kept him away from us, even though some stood no more than a few feet away. Until at last he stopped them one by one, and then, the last, smiled at us, and we all gave him a good hand.

It's here that I leave, or as I go back to it, this time, or this way, that is, now that I make my way out, through the rest of them, my hand on her arm with just that much pressure to guide her, or that is my intention. Perhaps the lights that make my eyes ache, begin to, or simply, that it's now, this point, that I am happy, that it's ourselves, the two of us, have come to some sort of feel of it, that makes us so. Just that I am, now, running, that it is just that I do.

What she had been doing, or going to that, it was a cigarette she asked me for, and I reached into my pocket for them, had got out the pack, and given her one, and then lit a match for her. She bent a little, got it lit, then looked back to the platform where the juggler had been.

But the trick, that it's him who's there, the midget, as such he is named, but the size, it's that which hits me, at first, that he isn't small, or looking, he must be five feet, or perhaps, a little smaller. Four feet. But not small.

The eyes, catch, get me so into it, that they are so, void, in the head, shaded, the shades like changing shadows, colors coming in to want, to want to be filled. Seem huge. He looks at all of us, moves over us so, to bite, to have something to be there to bite.

But nothing, certainly, to make of it more or more than what I could see, would be, that is, the barker introduced him, and we stood, as we had, in that group in front of him, the boards which made the platform, that roughness, and the poles on which the lights were strung, the wire sagging between them. That is, what is it had come in, as this was, to be not or to make it not as it had been, if it were, as it was, the same place, which I couldn't say or put my finger on, then, but waited like any of the rest.

I could see the muscle of his arm, where the sleeve had been pulled up, rolled, above it, and with his movement, that slightness of tension made him lift it, slightly, from time to time, the muscle tightened and it looked hard, big, below the roll of the sleeve. As my own would. He was smiling, the face somewhat broad, well-shaped, the smile somewhat dreamy, or like sleep, that vagueness, which couldn't be understood.

The barker had laughed, the pitch of it rolled out, on us, and I wondered if he was as drunk as he looked. He was calling the midget, cute, saying, a cute little fellow. He made a joke of it, looking at the women and laughing. Saying, who would like to take him home. There was laughing, they liked the joke, and he carried it further, sensing their tolerance, and played it up. It was the joke he seemed intent on making us remember, the cuteness, the idea of the women.

Taking the cigarettes out of my pocket, the pack crumpled, I held it out to her, but she was intent on what was before us, and I expect that I was myself, and only did what I did, took them out, to somehow break it, to make it break down. It seemed that, that is, that gesture or an act, an action, so meant to serve double, to be a break, but what was it, that is, more than the taking, just that, of the cigarettes, which I didn't want to smoke, had even just put one out. I looked, then, around me at the rest of them and they were looking at him, the midget, and I couldn't see one that noticed I looked, or gave the least sign.

The midget stood still, beside the barker, who staggered a little, under the lights, moved from one side to the other, his face to us, that drunkenness. He was still on the joke, fumbling, and it wore down on us, that weight of it, kept at us, and I wanted to get out. There seemed breaks, lengths of silence, hung there, made the other, the midget, the whole of it, in his own silence, which he kept as a distance around him, that the eyes made actual.

I would have gone, or as I think, I should have in spite of

it, simply slipped out, when the others weren't looking, just
left and waited for her outside. I can't see that she would
have been hurt. That is, I would think, or think I would
have that right to, that it would make no difference to her,
that is, that she would understand my going, seeing that it
had begun to tire me, even became painful to stay. I think
of it so, being such, that no difference could be in it, since
she was enjoying it, or so it seemed.

I tried to, but the people around pressed too tight,
pushed me from the back, all forward, to the one on the
platform in front of us. Not the barker, I knew that much,
but the other, who pulled them, kept them all, because the
barker had somehow fallen altogether to pieces, had just
the joke he hung on to, and that was played out. But then
he switched it, perhaps feeling it had, and turned to the
midget, and said, but you should have some say in this.
Which one would you like.

The midget turned, then seemed to pull himself out of it,
the distance, out of nothing, the eyes pulled in, to focus, to
grow, somehow, smaller, larger. The eyes went over us, the
voice, when it came, was breath, a breathing but way back
in, wire, tight, taut, the scream and I couldn't hear it, saw
only his finger move to point at her, beside me, and wanted
to say, he's looking at you, but she was turned away from
me, as though laughing, but struck, hit. I looked, a flash,
sideways, as it then happened. Looked, he looked at me,
cut, the hate jagged, and I had gone, then, into it and that
was almost that. But she said, then, she had seen him, earlier, that same day, as he was standing by a store, near the
door, I think, as it had opened, and she, there, across the
street, saw him motion, the gesture, then, a dance, shuffle,

the feet crooked, and the arms, as now, loose, and it was
before, as before, but not because of this, that made it, or I
thought, so made it, was it, or it was that thing I hung to,
when, the show over, they motioned us out, and I pushed a
way for her out through the crowd.

•

A Death

A
Death

Vestida con mantos negros
piensa que el mundo es chiquito
y el corazón es immenso . . . —LORCA

*A*head of them the path went round the trees, and into a clearing of stones, which had rolled from the higher points of the hill to make a sort of flat and broken plateau above the sea. Again, the children went in front, with Amos carrying the basket in one hand, and the other two crowding in back of him. She puffed at the cigarette for the last time, and dropped it, to step on it, and asked them all, how much farther it all was.

She was not a very pretty woman. Amos was six years old, and her one son. The facts sorted themselves like much too brief messages, not trivially but too quickly. She wanted to say something to the man now beside her, who was her brother, and his wife walked beside him on thick legs, wide and heavy at the ankles. Beginning to say it, she heard the children cry out, and there was Amos standing in the sun with the stone in his hand, in front of her, and then he threw it.

But that, at least, was not enough to bother them. James bound the wound, as he said, expertly, and soon the little girl had forgotten it, and ran once more after the others. The sun picked them out, in the shadows, and in and out they ran, around the rocks, and behind them, crouching, then waving the sticks again, and the parents sat in a small three-cornered circle watching them, and then looking at one another.

In her own head she now resolved, or arranged, a pattern of hostility, a final war against them, but that was her love for Amos. If he cried, that was too much. Or if he did not cry, but hit her, as he would and did, she would rather it were in their own room at the hotel, and not here in front of the others. He is a very nervous child, she said, his father makes no gesture of love to him. Or of affection.

So they pitied her. What was it like, they thought. What ever could it be like, in the heathen country of New Zealand. James said, he'll get over it. He laughed. His wife smiled at her, and she felt the edge of it coming in like the sharpness intended, to cut at her politely and to wound her. So she got up, and said she would take a little walk, calling Amos, and the two of them left and went down the hill to the sea.

As they grew smaller, the wife smiled again. James was uneasy, and their own children bored and impatient. He began to pile small stones, one very carefully on another, to build a small house. He made a door and two little windows, with small sticks for supports, and then the little boy kicked at it, and it fell to pieces.

In New Zealand, he said, but his wife would not listen to him. She took the children in her arms, one against each leg, and smiled again at him. He was the man she knew, and she would hear nothing at all to the contrary.

Closer to the sea the rock became sharper, and lifted into big, over-hanging bunches. A few pine trees grew somehow out of them, but these were very stunted, and low. The water was very lovely and very clear. One saw to the bottom. The fish moved out from the shallows, and seeing people come, disappeared altogether.

Amos was a fisherman. He had his own little pole, with a little reel on it, and would sit hours by the water without bothering her at all. Sometimes her husband came too. The first fish Amos ever caught, after many days and even years of fishing, was one which her husband had put on the hook for him, without him any the wiser. In a way it was sad that that had been the first, but after that he caught some actually.

Looking at Amos, she now wondered what she would change, if she could. His eyes were blue, almost shut in the intensity of their color. Perhaps he would be a great man in spite of them. His hair had bleached almost white, and under it the darker tawny color came through. But his arms were very thin and stick-like, and his chest corded with little muscles. He was like a goat, an obscenely precocious goat, who had no use for people.

Taking off their clothes, she put them in a pile, and then put a stone on top of it. Amos giggled. She had forgotten the bathing-suits, and they were in the basket, high up on the hill with the others. Even so she slipped into the water quietly, and calling softly to Amos, drew him in after her.

Above them, James fumbled in his embarrassment. His wife smiled again, and watching him, thought only of his remarkable innocence. It was pleasant that it should be so. He was very unmarked, and untouched by so many things. His sister might well be a photograph, she thought, which he wished to be proper and in focus. Otherwise she was a nuisance, as, for example, she paddled away down there, with the boy, and seemed almost completely foreign. James coughed, he wanted not quite to see. The bodies went under the water, to leave the heads free, then they too ducked under.

Still watching him, his wife said, what do you think of it, James. As she had said, three days earlier, to a young man on the beach with them, do you see how he treats me?

But what was so simple about it. Make me happy, she said. Don't please think of her. James was very much in the middle and began to know it. He knew love was not multiple, or could not be here divided. He said, be patient with her. He let it all rest on kindness.

The water around them changed all that, on their bodies, very much on their bodies. Amos jumped up, shrieking, and she loved him more than she admitted. Look, she said. The small fish darted out, past their white feet, and then back again to the darker places. But Amos had seen them. It was lovely.

Then she left him, swimming out, and free of it. The water was buoyant, so that she hardly swam but floated, lifted out on the wash of the waves as they fell back. Beneath her the colors changed from the green to blue, and then a darker blue, and then black. She dove and felt the tips of her fingers touch bottom, and on her hands the weeds were very light and brushed them gently.

Far away she thought that the house was now gone. Her husband loved no one anymore. At last they were also free

of him. He sat in a chair in the yard which he had made.
There was no car. The street was long, and at the end there
was a tram-stop. People spoke English but he answered
them, *no se*. He was a Greek with rings in his ears, and his
hands were folded in his lap.

So one could change it as he might. She held to that, and
here the water helped her, taking her as she was. One saves
all one's life, against the one instant it is all real, and all
enough. Why, she said, tell me now otherwise! Tell me
nothing.

If it is obscene, she said. Her husband's mother was obscene. Of her own husband she had known nothing, she
had not even known his body. And when at last he grew
sick, to die, she took off his clothes for the first time, and
saw the body for the first time, dying.

Gulls flapped off the rocks behind her. Amos slapped at
the water with a stick he had found. The quiet grew over
all of them.

But what was to be done with James. His wife thought
she knew, and yet he was strangely moved. The children
were happy, they played behind them with the toys they
had brought in the basket. So she attacked him directly,
and asked him, what was it. He said he did not know.

Is it your sister, she said, and looked down, and away, to
the form still clear to them, a white odd shape on the top of
the sea. He answered that he did not think it was. She said,
you must see the difficulties. He was not sure that he did.

But, corruption, she would have insisted if she had dared
to. The small knotted boy giggled at them, he caught at his
mother's skirt and giggled. She had neither sympathy nor
time for that horror. She has had a difficult life, he said.
And what is difficulty. He lifted the skirt, giggling at her

own children, he said to them, look. It was not possible to be kind.

To that James agreed, and yet it was still possible. The children played happily in back of them. The little boy threw the ball to the little girl. She missed it, and ran off to bring it back.

What do you think, his wife said. But a small boat now came into view, and he pointed at it, and they watched it crawl out past the rocks to their left, and then begin to come down the coast.

Hearing the sound of the motor, Amos looked up, and out. There it was, very white, with a little line of exhaust trailing the back. His mother was also out there, and he thought of it. He wanted the boat to take him away, perhaps to put him into the front somewhere, but he would never have the courage to go. He felt for a stone under the water, and found one close to his toes, and then threw it out as far as he could at the boat.

It missed the boat, but fell beside her, splashing her face. It was usual, and yet she looked back at him, in anger, to see him squatted there in the water, and, she thought, shivering. She wondered if the man, standing upright in the boat, could see her. He had seen the stone. His hand was on the tiller, his other let him lean back a little, braced against the boat's side. He was not tall, but he was strong-looking, his chest heavy. Now he did look, at first at the boy, and then coming closer, looked down and saw her as she took a stroke to swim back.

At that even James was angry. They had all expected it. She had only done what she would, but his wife was now right beyond all question. They watched the two figures collect themselves. The boat was no longer visible. Slowly they came up the hill again, and now it was impossible for James to swim, or for his wife, or children.

You know, his wife said, what this will mean. For the last minutes she wanted to be clearly fair. James watched his sister coming towards them, and saw her smiling. Was it to be a simple thing? She was not ashamed. Amos dragged at her hand, she pulled him along almost without realizing it.

Such a lovely swim, she said. The water was so lovely and refreshing. And the boat, the wife asked. But did she really say it. Her own children were safe behind her and never again would she really let them go. Amos giggled, he pulled at his mother's skirt, raising it, and James saw the tight thigh, and the brown, close flesh.

Did you see the boat, his wife said. She knew it was her brother's wife. She knew her own husband was dead. She saw the faces all in front of her, and if she cried out at them, she was still in love with everything.

•

3 Fate Tales

3
Fate Tales

1

I put it this way. That I am, say, myself, that this, or this feel, you can't have, or from that man or this, me, you can't take it. And what I would do, with any of this, is beyond you, and mine. But for this time, yours too.

I haven't always lived here. I used to live in the city, in the middle of it, straight, tall buildings, some of it, but where I was they were cramped, squat, four stories. There was a trolley-line ran down the middle of the street. Noise. Each day the iceman came, under the windows. I could hear him shout. I even waited for him to shout.

Thinking of that time, as it comes here, here and now, I think of the other, somewhat different. I say time. I say time, to mean place.

Let me put it another way. What have we got but this which is myself, yourself. Or that word, self. You figure there's more, some way to make it more, but what you keep is the means, the ways. Make them the end. And that's the end of it, what might have been more.

But nothing more strange, taken or not, than just that,

45

the self which is single. And I make it such, so call it, because it is so. I only call it what it is.

One day, any day, there could be these people, or make them three people, this man and this woman and this little girl. They live in the next place to mine. I see them go down the steps, out on to the street, there, the three of them. I don't say, look for yourselves, see them, or what you may take as enough to convince you. They are there. That is the fact of it.

The days are long, as it happens, hot. The sun in the city is a hard thing, up, inaccessible, hangs over the hardness of the city, out of it. Hot. I hate it but that is, again, my own business.

The woman sits there by herself, in the place with just the girl. They work out the day the best they can. Make the time pass. I know there are at least a hundred and one things anyone can do, to get through these days. Hold to, the actions, the little things done. I have my own things. I get up, eat breakfast, sit around, read, look out the window. There are these ways.

They wait, the two of them, in the place next to mine. The noises come through. The little girl has a ball. It bounces on the floor. Its noise is exact. The woman calls her for her dinner, she complains, doesn't want to come. There is some sharpness in the voices. I listen. I hear all that I want to hear of it.

Then, as it happens, there is this one day, again, one day out of the number, fifty, twenty-five.

The chair slides across the floor. I hear the girl push it.

There is no other sound. Just what comes comes up from the street, what I have grown used to, the trolley, and the cars, the people, below me, out the window, down. This is

what I am sure of, what is down there, that I can speak of
without looking, seeing, any of it. It is the one pattern
which cannot be broken because it is the general, the collection. The numbers.

It is still quiet. But then out, it goes by me, and down.
Stops. But I can't do anything, sit only for a moment, and
then, jump, and look out, see there, down, the girl and the
people already around her. Nothing of the woman until her
head is just opposite mine, the mouth wide, scream, and
someone I see the face of below, looks up and calls to her.
It's all right. She isn't hurt. A miracle.

It's all right, or right is what they have said, that it's all
right, but myself, I can't find their answers or even what
they answer, to say it's all right. To her, or myself, or anyone, or even looking straight down at it, after it happens,
what happens?

It isn't known. I make that sense of it, that it isn't known,
any of it. This woman or this girl or what has happened,
and how I would have it, or my hand there. To feel. To be
felt. Which they want, or I want, more than the seeing. Any
day of the week this could happen, to any, this girl, to
others, me, you. I suppose it is something, even, done with.
As it turned out. Past, and even complete. I am left with it,
made different, because of it. Or, am I? We are back to
that.

2

I take it another way, since in this or in what is around is,
perhaps, some of it, that such can come to interest, or finds,
so, some place in the attention. Let me begin.

There is an old woman who lives in the country and she
is very old indeed. Her husband, somewhat younger than

herself, has grown tired of waiting but being an honest
man, he cannot bring himself to the act of deciding just
how old she should be before she is ready to die. It is to be
thought that this old woman's days are inaccessible, even to
herself, and though she is certainly alive, for the most part
she is dead because she cannot remember anything and
when she talks, her words slide into one another and the
sentence breaks down before it is even half begun. It is a
practice of her husband, a rather cruel one, to have the old
woman do the week's shopping, so that each Saturday she
arrives in the village and totters from store to store, usually
led by some old friend of the family who has happened to
be standing on the street corner at the time when she is let
down from her husband's car. Often the job is divided so
that one begins it and then another goes on with it while a
third appears at the end to guide her to the car where her
husband sits waiting. And behind them comes the clerk
carrying the groceries. It is a common sight each Saturday.

This is, it can be supposed, one of the old woman's hor-
rors, but her joy, which is equally distinct, has to do with
something which for others would be even more horrible.
In the cemetery where she is, once dead, to be buried, her
stone is already set in place and her name with all but the
final date has been carefully cut into it. She is often taken
to the cemetery to see her stone, perhaps with a certain
willingness on the part of her husband who may think that
if she sees it often enough, this place where she is to be laid
to rest, she will hurry up the process of getting there once
and for all. For some years she worried about the possible
annoyance her choice of a final resting place might cause
another member of the family but when with reluctant de-

cision, she made her choice known to the family, she was overjoyed to find this doubtful one quite approved.

In any event this old woman seems to be doing it all by herself, so that when it does come time to bury her, one would not be too surprised, should the knotted old hands reach up and, pushing the shovels aside, pull the dirt over all by themselves, for at least that's one way to think of it.

3

I think we deal with other wisdoms, all more real than our own, which is to say, I think we have to do with others. Sometimes, sitting in a chair by the window, I see a man go by on foot and I wonder at the precision with which each foot advances, so controlled and so sure. I would hope that if the man and I were to trade places, he might think the same of me going by but I am not at all sure that he would.

I think it is always a question of where we have come from and where we are going. I think they are important in just that order and I think there is little else to think about. Of course, we are ourselves. It would be foolish for us to believe those who tell us different. But to know exactly, to know each time and all the time, about that I am not so sure.

After all, what do we have to do with that is not ourselves? What can exist that we are not part of or that we do not in some sense *allow* to exist. This is an old story but a true one. The world is my representation. So it is, all of it. And what is more, this world belongs to us.

But the order is important, the grasp of the keys and the lay of the land, so to speak. One must know these. Like the man with the•car I see each morning, racing its motor, tearing down the road over bumps and stones, what does he know about his own possession? Certainly not enough to make actual use of it, not the use of understanding. This, then, should be criticised, such misuse, and avoided at all costs.

But it is true that everything becomes our own. It's what things are for. We see them and they are ours. It's as simple as that.

The story I have to tell has to do with familiar objects in familiar relations. Unlike the others, it does not suppose a stretching of the usual context. It has to do with a usual reality.

I am in the habit of feeding our cat each night before I go to bed after I have put coal on the fires. This is my usual procedure and one I rarely vary. Both the cat and I are at home in it. When it comes time, if the cat is indoors, she will be sitting by her dish, waiting for me to put food in it. If she is outside, I have only to open the door and there she is, waiting to be let in and fed.

On the night of which I am speaking, or at least now I am speaking of it, I had let the cat out earlier and so when it came time to feed her, I went to the door and opened it but the cat was not in sight. But do not take this as something altogether unusual. I am not such an automaton that I cannot vary my movements at all. It is often the case that I am a few minutes late with the cat's food. And the cat, too, has her differences.

I opened the door but the cat was not to be seen, so I called to her, once, then twice, but she did not come.

On that night there was a full moon. It was very bright outside, almost like day but still very different. The tall pines at the edge of the field beside our house cast their long shadows over the snow and each object in the field itself that was big enough to have a shadow had its own. But though it seemed very light and the shadows black and distinct, still there were no sharp details such as are to be seen, when a bright sun is shining.

I stood for some minutes, looking out over the fields, and then, because she made a sudden, brief movement, I saw the cat not too far from where I was standing, crouched, her own shadow black and irregular on the snow. I called again to her but she gave no notice, so I walked over to where she was, thinking to pick her up and bring her into the house. When I came to her, however, I saw that she had a mouse and although it's no pleasant sight to watch a cat and a mouse together, one, in fact, which I remember always with unpleasantness, my wife and I have decided that since we have the cat in order to catch the mice which bothered us previously, we have to put up with the unpleasantness, even though it's difficult. So it was that I started to walk away from her in order to let her finish the mouse but as I did so, I was caught by the strange sight of their shadows, the mouse's, though smaller, very distinct and the cat's, like some horrible shadow trying to erase it. I stood there, absorbed, completely caught, until suddenly the mouse's shadow was gone, but no, it appeared again, coming toward me uncertainly, jerkily, until I saw that what it wanted was to hide in my own shadow, which I now saw to be there, just as their own, long and black on the snow. It came toward me, the mouse, and then just as quickly as I had seen it, I lost sight of it again. So again I started back to the house but as I did so, I felt something wriggling on my sleeve and with a sudden brush of my hand, I threw it back on the snow. Only then, because the cat jumped on what I had knocked from my sleeve, did I know it was the mouse.

I don't think that story much more than unpleasant but still it has the point of all I believe. For these things, so powerful in themselves, in their own way, are there to be looked at, I expect, and with more than the eyes. It's a case of making them ours the best way we can. I can remember that as it happened, then, even as it was happening, a good many things occurred to me, each with its relation, and if these things did, as they did, lessen that first impact of horror, they also made it my own.

There are other stories, some with more purpose, and one, perhaps, bears hearing here, tacked on though it is. In any event, it's short. After that snow and before the next, I went out, as usual, to do the chores, and found one afternoon, patches of blood on the snow. And seeing them there, I guessed that the cat had cut her foot and was able to find her and dress the wound before there was chance for it to become infected.

A short time after, it did snow and the patches were covered and I forgot about them. It stayed cold for a week and then it turned warm and the snow began to melt. And going out again I saw the patches of blood on the snow and without thinking twice, I went off to find the cat, supposing she had cut another foot. But finding her, I found, as well, that none of her feet were cut and then saw it was the melting of the snow had caused the old patches to come back. I expect that all this might suggest is that a reality, before it becomes our own, is often tricky and can be easily mistaken.

●

The Party

The
Party

Of uncleanliness, he was saying, there are, one must come to think, a good many kinds. Or more, put it, than dirt on the hands.

The wind shifted, slightly, pulling them down the lake and in toward the dock which he saw now as a line, black, on the water, lying out and on it.

Not one, he said, not one sense would give you the whole of it, and I expect that continues what's wanted.

But they sat quiet, anyhow, the woman at the far end, slumped there, and the length of her very nearly flat on the canoe's bottom. The man kept upright, the paddle still in his hands, but he held it loosely, letting it slap at the water, lightly, as the waves lifted to reach it.

Nothing important, she said. Nothing to worry about, and what about tonight? We forgot that.

He began to paddle again, but slowly, and looked back at her reluctantly, almost asleep.

That doesn't please you, she said. You seem determined not to enjoy yourself.

Not that, he answered, and it had taken him, at that, some way beyond where he had been.

Not so simply, he said. You make it too easy.

But why easy, she answered. I don't see that it's not easy, any of it. These people will hardly care to attack you personally. They are all much too busy.

Looking down at her, he found her laughing at him, and smiled himself.

You are all so very serious, she said, all of you. What is it makes you think the world is so intent on you at whatever age you are.

Because I don't know, she added, just how old you are. But you look young. You look very young.

He whistled, a little song, and looked back toward the dock which they now came to, bumping against it, and he reached out to steady them, and then pulled the canoe alongside for her to get out.

Easy, she said. Don't jerk it.

He watched her swing out, a foot on the dock, then pull herself up, and clear, to wait for him.

Help me pull it up, she said. It might break loose.

He got out and helped her lift it, and then pushed to roll it over, on the dock, easing it down gently, when her hands were clear.

There, she said, now it will be safe.

He followed her back along the dock, crossing at the end, another, and then up a path to where her car sat, shaded, by the trees. She opened the door for him, and reaching in, spread a towel on the seat, then crossed round to the other side. Sliding under the wheel, she leaned over and caught him with one hand, pulling him to her, to kiss him.

For your sullenness, she said, although you hardly deserve it.

He pushed free and watched her start the car.

Sometime you will have to answer me, she said. Sometime there will be nothing else for you to do.

They moved off quickly, along the road, and coming to another, swung in, grating, and up to the house, and stopped there and got out.

Leaving her, he went to his room, took off his bathing-suit and dropped it on the floor. To his right a mirror hung, on the wall, and he turned to look at himself, the whiteness, and then dressed quickly, and left the room.

Here, she called.

The voice echoed a little, finding him, and he followed it out to where she was sitting, waiting for him.

There's not too much time, she said. Would you like a drink before we go?

He nodded and she got up, and went out. Returning, she came to him and put the glass on the small table by his hand. Then she went back to her own chair and sat down.

Thanks, he said, and picked up the glass from where she had put it.

But nothing at all! Very happy to do it.

He smiled, then drank, and put the glass back.

This is a very comfortable room, he said. Very airy, very nice and big.

She nodded, quiet, and looked round at the walls, the high ceiling, then back at him.

He wanted it this way, she said. He did most of it himself.

He looked away, turning, and settled on a picture which was across from him, a small one of some trees and a house.

His favorite room, she said. This and the shack were all he cared about.

A damn shame, he said, to have just got it, and then to have to lose it.

She didn't answer, and looked, instead, out the window, her head somewhat bent, and loose, and he watched her, quietly, letting the time pass.

It makes me feel rather dirty, he said, rather stupid, if that's how to say it.

It's not you.

But it must be me a little, he said. That I walk in on it.

You don't. There's nothing to worry about.

She had got up and now looked at her wrist, the little band there, of some bright metal, and then at him, saying, it's very late.

He followed her out and into the car, and starting it, she drove off quickly, hurrying because of the lateness. Some cars were already there and they pulled in behind them, and stopped.

It won't be bad, she said, or it won't be if you'll try to help a little.

He shrugged and went after her up the path, waiting behind while she knocked, lightly, on the door. Abruptly it opened and he saw a woman smiling at both of them, reaching, to pull them in. He let them talk, standing back, and then went in after them.

You're the last, the woman said, but that's an honor?

Yes, she said, and they went in, closely, following the woman, laughing, and he saw them all sitting in a ring about the room, the chairs all back against the wall, and going to one near the door, he sat down.

Mr. Briggs, they said, and all laughed, is a strange young man!

But he had not heard them, and only sat, placid, and

again waited for a drink, thinking it enough that there should be one for him. It came soon and taking it, he thanked the woman and lifted the glass to his mouth.

Cheers!

He sat back, more relaxed, and nodding to the man beside him, said, very fine, and smiled.

There's not much hope for them, the other answered, if they won't make an attempt to see both sides.

No, he said, I can't see that they will find any other way out of it.

But it doesn't matter, she asked. Who could care about such a thing.

The sandwiches went by him, and reaching out, he caught one, smiling, and put it into his mouth.

The truth, the other said, is what rarely seems to be considered.

But they had not heard either, and one woman now stood up, and looked at all of them, saying, to John. Wherever he is. They drank in silence. A windy void, which he felt himself, lifting the glass, and drinking, then, with all of them. It was love, she said, a very true love.

From the next room the children's voices came, clearly, and they were crying, wailing, he thought, with a very specific injury. Getting up, he said, I'll go, not thinking, and had gone through the door before anyone had noticed him.

But, seeing him, they cried louder, screaming, and the woman was there behind him, and motioned him out.

But no, she said, it's no use. You bad children, go to sleep!

Bewildered, he looked down at her, beside the bed, and younger than she who he had come with, he thought, but she will not allow me, she will not understand.

We'd better go back, she said. They'll go to sleep by themselves.

In the other room they had got up, and stood only to wait for her, to say, goodnight, apologetically, and left. She watched them go, blankly, and he stood beside her, trying, as he thought, to help.

My party, she said. There's no reason to leave.

It's late, someone answered. It's been very fine.

The room cleared, slowly, the doorway crowded but at last empty, and they sat, the three of them, on the couch, looking after the others. In the room behind them the crying continued and softened, finally, to die out.

They're all asleep, he said, and turned, but could not see her face.

Does it matter, he said. I mean, does it matter in any way you can think of?

But the woman had got up, and the other now raised herself, to lean over, and seeing him, laughed, and sank back.

You make it sound momentous, she said. You really prefer disasters.

She smiled at him quickly, lifting again, but he had turned his head and she could not see him.

Anyhow, it was a good party, she said then, turning to the younger woman. There was certainly nothing wrong with it.

The Lover

The
Lover

Outside, beneath the window on the grass which grew in an uneven covering, the earth coming through in patches where the grass had worn thin, the cats were playing. The sun was as high as the noon would find it and yet the air had an edge of chill in it and the sky was a yellow-blue, the chill, and hardness. It was summer but they were north, so far north that even the summer was part of it, cold and not the open warmth of the south which they had grown used to a year ago, that they had travelled in with the cats as unwelcome retainers, servants of their love. They had need for an audience.

At noon the glasses and sandwiches sat on the table, and they before them, and they both ate without haste, or eagerness, but more as occasion, usual, for which there was custom. Still, looking at them, together, it was to catch some of the reason for them being together. There seemed to be a reason. She was short and he was tall and both were somewhat dark with brown hair, eyes, rather oval, long faces, and then their bodies, having some sense of strength in them, and one thought that they would look better without the clothes than with them. There was too much awkwardness and constraint, although one might have been mistaken.

Too much subtlety, he was thinking, altogether, to want much to eat today. He said, I've been reading about this new book here. It says, that *his unwavering growth is continuing*, that he *has been achieving universal recognition as a master craftsman of the very first order*.

Taking another sandwich, he said, what has happened to my generation? Tell me. Where are those that stood with me?

And she answered, looking up above his head through the window, to the peak of the barn: Isadore, shot in a raid, 1938; Leo, serving 2 years for addiction, 1944; Sarah, teaches dancing in New York, 1948—those are the ones that matter.

When will they call me, he said, when shall I resume my command?

But she was clearing the table and then she had gone into the kitchen, leaving him on the chair, still sitting, and he looked at the door and then turned to look out of the window and saw there the black and white cat, with a mouse, while the other, the grey cat, sat some distance away, watching.

Poetically, he was an instance of despair, one more, as he would put it, in the noon's sun. He could plan himself out of books or without them, what he could do but couldn't then get to it or come to it. He thought of Sarah as a body, before him, which he would put out hands to touch, or fingers to move over. That would be a body, he thought, love. Was she one of those mentioned? She was. She is dancing in New York, although where wasn't mentioned. Would she dance well? He thought, I guess she would. I guess that would be love, another instance, dancing or not. But the others, that would be more subtle.

He spent that afternoon cleaning out a hen-house, moving the caked litter in a basket to the truck, then taking it when he had got the house cleaned to the dump at the edge of the woods. It wasn't hard work so much as dusty, and his nose was blocked with the dust and he coughed now and then. But it had to be done, he thought, but will they remember it five years from now.

And then it was evening and he could sit down again, at the table, and eat his supper. He ate it fast and with appetite, and she was pleased. After they had finished, he went into the other room, she before him, and sat down again in the chairs some feet apart. He took up the book he had been reading in the morning, opened it, then shut it and put it back. His wife had one of her own which she had begun to read.

I think I'll go to New York, he said, and then waited. She went on with her reading. I think I'll leave tonight. She put the book down and looked at him, but annoyed and even hurt, and this surprised him. Go ahead, she said, but there isn't any money. I'll walk, he said, I'll run, I'll fly. Go ahead, she said. But why get angry, he said, why take it that way? What is here to keep me? And why won't you come? I don't like New York, she said.

It was there he could stop, he thought, right there. To hell with it. Women with bodies but each different and each with incomparable differences and each with exciting differences. But I'm a lover, he thought, good god, this is my vocation. You fat, stinking hag!

Around the edge of the chair one of the cats came and pushed against his foot, rubbing itself on his leg, and purring. He put down his hand and stroked its back, slowly, so that his fingers could feel the fur very soft and even and almost like oil, very thin, on the fur. The cat purred and arched its back, then tired of being stroked and moved over to where his wife sat and jumped up to her lap, landing on the book and covering it. Annoyed, she pushed it down.

Outside, down in the field, there was a mist coming up from the river which he could still see in what light was left. It softened the outlines of the trees, covering them, and what he could now see of them was not the trees, but the mist covering the trees.

A softness of the world.

Sentimental and odious.

But what could he put against it, he thought, that it hadn't got to and covered? A softness of the world. A vacuum, an impenetrable emptiness. Two years ago he had been in New York with Leo and Sarah. They had stayed at Leo's apartment. Leo wanted Sarah. It was what he wanted, her, that is, but still the idea of having some one, that being what he had mentioned later. I was so alone, he said, having no one to sleep with. So what did you do. He didn't know, he thought, then or now, not much in any event. I've never done much of anything. But Leo said, you slept with her. Which was right, but that was up to her, and he could think of her in the bed, after, when he had got up to go back to his own, saying, she said, stay with me, don't go back, and he felt her face because he was obliged to see what she was up to and found there that she was crying, the tears coming down over her face, and he stayed where he was. And when Leo asked, he told him. How old, he thought, 23, 24, and still I can't keep my mouth shut? And old men talk too much?

He saw her moving in her chair and he sat up, quickly
and straight, in his own. You've been asleep, she said. But
he couldn't think that he had been, or remember, and answered, no, that would be too easy and too right. I haven't
been asleep. I watched you, she said, and you fell asleep.
She was smiling and why should she have to smile. What
did you dream about, she asked, and smiled. Women, he
said, nothing but women. Nice ones, she asked. You don't
know them, he said, and tried to remember what he had
dreamt about, but couldn't. But he thought, was I asleep,
and, where am I now?

Whose room with such impossible furniture is this? The
cat lay in a corner of the room, the one that he had stroked,
curled on a blanket that lay there, the other close to it. So
where am I, he thought, is it still 1938? What year is it if it
isn't 1938?

He said to her, I don't do anything but think, do I? She
had got up and was going out to the kitchen to feed the
cats. She hadn't heard him. He tried again. I don't do a
goddamn thing, but think, do I? She was in the kitchen and
he wondered if she heard but didn't answer because she
didn't want to. Why don't I work, he shouted, why don't I
get a job? Good Christ, who do I think I am? Sitting around
here all day doing nothing? Look at other people. They
work. They have jobs. They support their wives. Why don't
I?

It was very quiet in the house, he thought, and now that
he had stopped shouting, he could hear her in the kitchen,
getting the cats' food. No noise from the night came into the
room and looking out, all he could see was the black and
the quiet. Nothing moved. Stop thinking about it. Get
out of it. Let go. But the women are there, he thought, all

of them, one, two, three, four, five. Were there that many?
No, he thought, there weren't. But there could be, there
might be even more. As a possibility he could add a half a
dozen, to begin with, that he knew of and could, perhaps,
someday add. That would be a beginning. But what com-
pels me here?

How about some music, he called to her. She was still in
the kitchen, feeding the cats. Some big wide chords? He
waited and then she answered, don't you want to go to bed?
No, he said, I'm not tired. Let's have some music. He got
up and went over to the phonograph. Reaching down to a
rack below it, he pulled out an album, very worn and
patched on the sides with tape. He took out three records,
put them on the spindle, joggled them a little to make sure
they would drop down one at a time, and then turned on
the phonograph. In a minute the sounds came out, loud,
deep, and fast. He moved out to the middle of the room,
stood there, listening, and then let his arms swing out in
lazy circles, easy, and murmured to himself the sounds of
the music. When it had finished, he turned around to find
her standing in the doorway, smiling again, and watching
him.

You look like Buddy, she said, but not very much. That's
one you forgot, he answered, what about him? Where is
he? He's in Mexico, she said, but you know that. He looked
at her in the doorway and wondered. I know it, he said, but
do you know it? Do you know what it means to me, for
example? I think so, she said. No, you don't, he said, I do
but you don't. Wait a minute. He walked over to a table
and took a letter from a small pile on one side. Listen to
this. He unfolded the paper and read, *que nunca olvidate*
. . . , he says here, *Your lad que nunca olvidate* . . . He

had trouble pronouncing the Spanish and she asked him to spell out the words. What does that mean, he said. It means, which nothing will obliviate. Nothing, he said, how does he get that way? What does he know about it down there in Mexico? Don't you like him, she said. But he turned and folding the letter again, put it back on the table with the others. I like him, he said, very much.

She had gone over to the door and opening it, she looked at him, to see if he was going to come, but he went back to a chair and sat down and said that he would read for a little while. Take a bath, I'll be up soon. I haven't much to read. Then she was upstairs, moving around, turning the water on in the tub, and no other sounds but these. He took up the book again, opened it, but couldn't read it, and closing it, put it back on the table. Too often, he thought, I've done that. Too goddamn often these days. But thought then that what he would like would be no more than something obscene, of the sort that he could remember having got hold of as a boy, in school, but this was usual. But for a grown man, he thought, is it still usual?

Upstairs he found her still in the tub, stretched out, and almost asleep. He had left the door open as he came in and she complained of the cold draught from the hall, but he left it open long enough to annoy her and wake her up. Or perhaps no more than to annoy her. He didn't know. Then he closed it and stood waiting for her to get out of the tub, but she stayed where she was and he looked at her there, in the dirty water, grey, so that he couldn't see her under it but only what was above, her breasts, head and knees. My wife, he said, look at you, you big, common thing. Get up or you'll go to sleep. She smiled and then slowly started to get up and the water slopped against the sides. He didn't wait but went out, closing the door behind him, and into their bedroom, and there undressed, and putting on his pyjamas, got into bed.

Another book on the table, he thought, and there it was. Books everywhere, he thought, nothing but books. It was another he'd been reading with a torn match-book in it to mark the place where he had stopped. He reached down to his pants which lay where he had dropped them on the floor, took out a package of cigarettes and a lighter. He lit one of the cigarettes and then put the pack and the lighter on the table beside the bed.

Then she was in the room and looking up at her, he saw she'd let her hair down and had put on lipstick, so that her mouth looked bigger. Just like those books, he thought, and she said, I'm all clean, do you like me? She got into the bed and rolled over against him and began to stroke him with her hand, her hair falling over his chest, and he said, look, what do you think I can do, what do you think I'm good for. But he was getting excited, himself, and he reached over and with his hands, took hold of her.

But who is it, he was thinking, that I would want if it wasn't her? But would this be important now? He wondered. He wondered if it were, then, those projected images of other, those other, women he was dealing with, then, in the bed with her, on top and around her, and over her. Or if it were himself, or where was he in it. Like some kind of impotent shell, useless to protect, he thought of the day and the sun and the lack of warmth, the north, being that climate he had no business in, too cold and hard, around him and over, on top, and talk, damn you, talk, he thought, say something, that makes sense, that won't leave me always alone, here or there, or nowhere I have chosen

for myself, as I am now, here or there, but nowhere I would
be. And the cats, he thought. The shell. The need for necessity, to have dependents. She liked them, she fed them.
They were hers. And it was useless not to be angry anymore because he was and expected he would be, for a long
time, that it would continue to be her that he didn't want or
like or didn't want to have close to him, and always busy,
he thought. Always busy. And could, then, scream, get
away from me, you common thing! But she had rolled off
and away, or he had, and lay there thinking, what was I
thinking of.

In the Summer

In the Summer

I am not saying that it was ever to the point or that a purpose could be so neatly and unopposedly defined. Or that twenty-one or so years ago, on that day, or on this, he was then, or is now, there or here, that we could know him and see him to be what he is. I don't much care for that. I had my own time to do, a number of things to do. I had heard, then, that the growing-up of anything could become an involved and crippling process. I could see the sun each day, coming up, and then each night, going down. I gave my time to that.

She said: do you really believe that, do you really see things that way.

Of course, it isn't so neat, he said. He was being somewhat difficult, he thought, to allow her to speak of things which didn't have to do with her, but her hands, in his own, were chafed, and rough, and his own, moving over them, in a kind of tired realization that they were not what they might be, said, here's a little warmth, take it.

No, I couldn't have to do with him, then, because I was afraid of him, of having him come too close to me, or to himself, for that matter. I knew then what I was, what gave me pleasure, or how I should best set about getting it. It was no sin, to know that. I got up early in the morning, each day, to get that jump on everyone else. They didn't see that I did, but just the same, I did.

So is love, in itself, a kind of inverse plunging, which I cannot say more about, or much more, than that.

She said: why love, what has that got to do with this, what you were saying about him.

And withdrew, a little, her hand from his hold which was to say to him, that she had become suspicious and was now thinking of something else. But he drank what beer he had left in his glass and took that occasion for speech, finishing.

Like that, he said, that I was then thinking of it, the beer. That was what I had in mind. And I could love that too, I expect. One thinks of hot days and it's not so hard then.

She said: but not the same way.

The same way, he said, no different. And that is what was wrong then. Wanting to give. That is itself a sin. There is no other sin that I can think of that is worse. And I should damn it more thoroughly, than I could myself, for considering it or any one thing. That I haven't the time for, now or then.

The question would be always the same in love, and is: can it be taken. How can I best take hold of it, in what multiple ways, and all of these with the obscenity of blindness. Since it will never be what I take.

She said: this is all the same, I know all this, and the kind who say it.

And he could not himself have made such a thorough round comment, as she had made, for which he didn't so much as remember, later, that she had said it but forgot then, in himself, that she was even there, or that he again

had her hand, the fingers of which he went over, one by
one, counting, making sure.

What summer is more beautiful, he began, and then began again. What summer is more beautiful than the one I
can tell you about. Let us think of it as all orchards and
that kind of smell, a freshness there, which one couldn't
lose hold of if one wanted. From the house, between the
single row of maples that stretched down over the slight
hill to the field below, it was always to be going somewhere
far from the house though I could be called to it by even
the slightest of voices, to come back for whatever it was
they wanted. And close to the top of this hill I had my
coops, for my pigeons, and they were all different colors,
different shapes. On the windy days I would let them out,
with the clouds, and they would go up, very high, except
for those who could not quite get there or loop in long fast
circles, but would hang in the air, to wait for the others to
come round or back, and then would start off, as leaders,
only to be left again, and to wait. These were my fantails,
which were awkward, strutting birds, with wide spread
tails. Mine were white and one spring I had a very nice one
but he wasn't banded and so he was never worth very
much to anyone but myself. But that is another tragedy,
and not this one.

We spent that summer at home and when my mother's
vacation came, we didn't go anywhere, to the beach or up
to the mountains, but stayed there in the town. I expect
that I was a little sorry then, but not too much. I had any
number of birds that year and could not be got very far
from them, except to see someone else's, which got me
about, at least a little, here and there, to see the other boys
of my age, or the men who had not got beyond this time in

their own lives and whose garages or houses still sprouted
with flycoops and a variety of pens. It was something to do.

He had left the first part of that summer, to go to a camp,
a caddy-camp, some distance away, at a big hotel, in the
mountains, which his father thought would be good for
him, to learn to take it, and to make a little money. He was
somewhat stronger than myself, a year older, so in that way
he went, without thinking much of myself or that it was
strange that I didn't go too. Another year I was to have
gone, he said. I would go, as it had then been agreed. But
for myself, I missed him very much, the first part, and
would get cards from him, these not very often, and pain-
fully written, as a fifteen-year-old boy will write to one a
year younger than himself, in a way that neither can understand, being fragments thrown off from the very force of his
living. I wrote to him much the same things as we had been
doing when he was at home, that such and such had come
or gone, these all on the only postcards I could get, of the
town-hall, looking very grey and shoddy against the hard
geometry of the square with the surrounding and enclosing
stones. It was not wrong, then, to consider myself, in spite
of the summer's warmth, and what I had to do with it, still
abject and though I could not then have thought so, pa-
thetic.

Sometimes I would go down to the barn which his father
had moved and built again, by himself, though we boys
gave what help we could, to be doing something during the
fall he put it up. And there it was, then, and maybe now,
what tribute he could put into so much wood, for his son,
that he could move and put up again with his own hands,
to put the pony in, which he couldn't afford, yet would
have. I was allowed to ride the pony that summer, now and

then, when he was around but he fed it while his son was away, and would let no one else do very much for it. So for most of the day it was staked out, like a cow, under the apple trees for shade though not so near to any of them that it would eat the apples and get sick.

The barn wasn't too big, just room enough for a good-sized box stall and what hay the pony ate during the winter, and a place for harness and saddle. And he hadn't finished it off altogether, being in a hurry as he was to get it done, so the pony could come, and only himself to do it. So a good number of the boards were nailed with only a single nail in the corners where the pony wouldn't go, though where the stall was and the way out to the main door he had fixed with two-by-eights, double-planked, which the pony would never break through.

A year before the boy and myself had hit upon one board in particular, soon after the pony came, when we were down in the barn, most of the time, that we lifted and put things under, pushing them far back, as far as we could reach, cigarettes and what else we had.

And reaching under there, then, that summer, I could get hold of the corner of the magazine and pull it out, without tearing the page I had got hold of, slowly, dragging it, and then the book, with the back off and the pages mildewed from having been under there so long. And on the first page could see the woman under the slightness of the slip, with its fine line of cloth covering only that much of the breasts which would have been in itself enough for the hand of a fourteen-year old. And where the cloth moved down the body against the flesh, to the leg, and there stopped, to end in a kind of torn edge, against the flesh, which I knew almost by heart, and then to the face, with the look of kind, that kind of, dismay, which then explained the man with his own face, in the picture, across from her, but coming closer, with his hands stretched out and wanting, about to, tear off the slip.

Or the book, which I can, perhaps, still quote, being those pages which I have no right to forget, or not quite so quickly, since it was there written, that '. . . she did not at first understand what he expected of her. But he came closer and then she knew that he was about to . . .' As I myself was.

At least this much we had stored against a time when we should know more of it, that those pages should themselves secure us, that we should then know, all. But not enough then, to see what we were cheated of. Those times I came alone, that summer, to the barn, perhaps, what was I looking for, and here I am very near tears, or much closer than you may think, to look at me. That I should somehow have expected his own words to have been there, on the edge of the page, which would have been meant for me.

What embarrasses here is not altogether what you think but is that which will always be more sad than embarrassing. I am not sure that I speak now, even for myself, that I have not become the fact of much more than I intend. But I do speak of myself, nonetheless.

With the end of summer or toward the end of summer, since it had not quite come but only that slight feel of the days somewhat faint and beginning to go into another kind of color and tone, with that time I began to look for him to come home again, from the camp. Later I read of those fair lovers who lay, without sleep and all cares, on those no harder beds than love's own caring, but then I could not invoke them. That much you must understand. I had no idea of what part I should have in anything, much less in this. So he came home one day toward the first of September, with his father in their car, and drove into the yard opposite ours which was where he lived then, in a small white house, Cape Cod, as they call them, to which his father had added some dormer windows and inside, rooms, so that there would be places for them all. I could see them getting out of the car and then the bags and boxes coming out of the back, with all his things, and then I expect I wanted to go over and help, but didn't, and instead went down to the barn, since I knew he would come there, soon, to see the pony, if it was all right after the summer and his being away from it.

She said: he came.

He came, he said, but it wasn't sad. There was nothing there or in that that got me, then, and it wasn't until later that I got what I should have got there. It had been strong enough apparently to carry the summer with it, all that fine weather, into the colors of the fall, the cold, and then all that winter, sometimes in his house, sometimes in mine.

She said: what had you expected from any of it, being fourteen as you were, or any age, for that matter, what was it you wanted to get out of something like that, that you knew you couldn't, and didn't, later, much want, but just then wanted, as though you knew that later it would have to come to me, this kind of thing, to ask me what I thought and did I understand, as if there, in any of it, was what I was supposed to understand.

I don't know, he said, since then or there I haven't been for sometime. Sometimes it is just that I can't remember any of it or have like a kind of fog that which I felt then, to wonder about, and to put against, even, what I have now.

She said: you haven't anything, even with him here, it's yourself you care about, and want, that you can hurt both of us, or I don't care about him, if it's what you want me to do, that I shouldn't care.

The Seance

The
Seance

Somewhat colder, the wind came in at the door, and with a quick turn, shifted and moved down the hall. There, they were sitting, waiting, at the table, backs to the fire, the shadows of them on the wall, against it, big black shapes there which, because they were talking, they didn't see.

A ghost story. An involution back into what was, he said to the other, remember? I give it to you straight, listen.

You see the face, say, that face there. What is it gets on it, I mean, the fact of it coming over & thru, now, as you are looking. Or, how it dies, perhaps, or softens, the thing gone relaxed, like a dying. My hands are cold. I move them a little, flex & wind the fingers together. The coldness. Or rub them, perhaps, one with the other, chafe the skin a little. A charm against what harms them. The coldness. Not so much to laugh at this, or to be laughing, as to see, simply, what it is I am about.

Perhaps, then, in some ways something, something different. Someone is moving. The chair, itself, edges a little, & grates, the legs of it, against the floor. Listen. Unmistakable sound. The slight shifting. The slight noise in the ear. Enough to prove it. Something there. Well, someone. A person, like they say. Man, woman, or child. Who is cold? Not so much cold, as there. That is itself a character.

But even with that, it is still not there, or better, it is away from where we are. Where I am. Or put it simply. I am alone.

To move from this to that. That shift, from here to there where the weather is softer, warmer, & the sun already grows big against the edge of the hills, where the eye hangs, to look at the sun, against it. Strikes out. The trees, green but soft green in the rising fog which the rising wind pushes. He said, never a morning without the slight wind. Clears this fog, cuts thru & lifts it, clears sight.

So good to be stretching. Out, lifts over the edge of the bed, one leg, looks down at the foot, then gets up. Stretches. Through the window, the sun works clear & up, moves higher, & the air is warm.

Lucy sings in the garden, two hours before him, gropes for the weeds, is mad. Tra-las, echoing song. Lifts high as the sun these symptoms of the desperate sound. Weeds, where they grow, catch to her flowers & crowd. She, meticulous, takes each, one by one, carefully, & pulls, lightly, works them loose. The flowers. Color & the morning sun.

Not much more than that, he was saying, I was thinking, again. My head feels thick as a bag of barley. Thick? Well, barley not so much that as slippery. That too, in my head. What was it you wanted to know about—let's get clear on that. At this point it's hard to think straight. I'm in a hurry.

Colder & colder. He rubs his hands more frequently, puts them to his mouth & blows on them, thru. The warm breath. Is uncomfortable & the fire burns out. But flickers. The shadows even more.

The sun, higher & higher. The day burns out. Along. And

she is still in the garden, still pulls at the weeds. Which move thru her hands. Counters. Lucy, green, Louise, green. Lionel, green. Lilacs, purple. Purple. Moves her hands with exactness, picks & pulls.

Behind her, thru a chink in the wall, he is watching. Takes after a time, a small pebble & throws it, tosses it, at her. It hits her back & bounces, lightly, down. She shakes & keeps working. He takes another pebble, & throws it, she shakes & keeps working. Another. Throws. She keeps working. Another, larger, throws, harder, another, larger, throws & harder another. She keeps working.

The whistle, far-off, a kind of long screech. All over, they stop. Put down the tools & move in long lines, past the tools & out. A digression.

But the wind shifts, again, comes down the hall, and finds him. Close to the fire, what's left, he puts his hands out to catch what heat is left. Cold, very cold. No moon but out on the fields the weather. Light light. He rubs his hands.

The Grace

The
Grace

*F*rom somewhere else he could hear it, but the crying at least had stopped, and turning, he saw her at the door, shutting it quietly, and putting a finger to her lips.

Quiet, she said, and came in, then, to sit down in the chair opposite him, sinking down there and letting her legs go out, slack, in front of her. Behind him he had put the candle and it burned, flickering, but a light, and as soft as any he might hope for.

Otherwise, there was a moon, and this rose, very gently, somewhere back of the house. The road looked a liquid, or water there, translucent. He felt it as pleasant, perhaps, but was too tired to get up and at her suggestion, that they might walk, said, no, and slumped back.

There was no time, he said, but knew she had another sense of it. Something, he said, makes a mess of it.

She got up to light another candle and put it on the table behind him, but bitterly, he thought, and watched her sit down again.

We can hope for another place, he added. This is just for the time-being. Call it a vacation, or anything like that.

But the house, or the rooms, something bothered, and she

had little peace, accepting nothing of it, and moving with a kind of rigidness through it all. Now she got up again, impatient, and lighting the stove, began to heat water for the dishes.

Can I help, he said, when she looked at him, but she turned away again, and he relaxed.

Outside it grew light, or seemed to, almost like day, but whiter, again that translucence, and he wondered if out there one might not be another thing altogether, even though it should seem otherwise. To the west were some small lights, single, each a small brightness, and separate from the rest. He imagined gaiety, or even singing; the tables of some place packed and people altogether without malice. He thought it might be like that, and felt, too, the moon was the sign.

She had cleared the table, taking the dishes to the sink, to put them at the side, and then filled the sink with the water she had heated. Meticulous, in some sense, she washed them one by one, to put them down again, again at the side, until they were done. Then left them there, to dry by themselves.

Sitting down, she looked up at him, and waiting, she reached over to pick up her knitting, and then began, the needles very bright, and quick, in her hands.

But he had started, and spoke, now, of what he had thought himself to have forgotten, a picnic so long ago it seemed inconsequential, though he could not have said, then, why. Somewhere his grandmother had carried out the lemonade, or he remembered it, in a bright tin pitcher, to place it on the long table, under the trees.

It should be like that, he said. What do we give of that,

or what do we try to. Tell me one thing we do that is as nice as that.

She hadn't answered, but anyhow he assumed her attention, and wanted to make it clear.

A fine old lady, he said. I mean, really. She knew what work was, though I suppose she minded, certainly. That it couldn't have been very pleasant for her.

I don't suppose it was, she said, and looked at him.

Or that other, the one the old man told us about, his mother, who died by the window there, took three drags on her pipe and then slipped out. How about that!

She laughed, herself, and found it simpler, the time less persistent, and had gone back again, with him, and sat in the old room, as she supposed the old lady had, lifeless, and in the dark.

That was in our house, she said. In the living-room, by the back window. He said she used to knit there too, in the moonlight.

One would like to go back, he had said. One would rather not move away ever, or go anywhere but where one was.

Even so, the moon rose, higher, and now came clear through the door they had left open, and came across the floor very softly, to touch the back of his chair. He grew quiet, sinking down, and pushed out his legs, reaching her, one foot against her own.

From somewhere above the boy cried, whimpering, and putting down the knitting, she got up, to cross to the stairs, and then he heard her go up, the crying continuing, and growing louder. He started to get up himself, but sat down, annoyed, and wondered what the matter was, calling to her, to hear her answer, nothing.

Echoes, he thought. But the crying grew less, then stopped, and soon she was back, and sat down again across from him.

He was frightened, she said, and seeing him angry, added, he isn't settled yet.

The anger went, and left him lost in some other thought, of the house, and where they had been, call it, in another place.

He must miss it, he said. But there it is, I mean, one moves anyhow? And stopped, to say, isn't it? Isn't that what has to happen?

I don't know, he said, insistent. I don't know why it is so much place with them. Not that I don't get it, that is, don't get what moving does to a kid, but what else? We've been here close to two months.

She let him go on, and sat only there, silent, and not with any malice. Hard to believe it otherwise, or he wondered, then, if it could be otherwise. Something he thought of as impenetrable, but getting up, he asked her to come out, saying he felt like a walk now, if she still wanted to.

She followed after him, and they started off down the road, past the other houses, close, and then off through the fields, the moon there very much a whiteness and lying on the ground with grace. He said he could not really believe it. That it was, then, a world so very close to their own.

But it is here, he insisted, and took her arm to hold it. It has to be?

They went on, following the edge of the field, the ground rough and uneven under their feet. Now and again she stumbled, and he held her up, and at last they sat down there on the grass, and lay back.

Straight up, above them, the moon was beginning to slip, and sink down, but shone with a fierceness, and made them seem bluish to each other, hands looking pale and unreal.

She had raised herself, a little, then leaned on him, over, and her hands took his own, lightly, as she kissed him. But he had not stopped, or only for that instant, and looked up at the distance above him, saying, he didn't know, and felt the ground hard under both of them.

It's all right, she said, and moved to stroke him, hoping to help, to ease it. One knows that it will be.

He rested, and felt her fingers very careful, finding him with a certain gentleness, or that sure. He said, thanks, and laughed a little, lifting to take hold of her, but they heard the faint crying, from the house, coming after them, and got up.

She went ahead, running, and he called to her to be careful, then saw her reach the road. From somewhere another sound, a cry, rising, to die out. He tripped and fell down, sprawling, and got up again, rubbing his knee.

Coming in, he found it quiet, and she was sitting in the chair by his own. He looked toward the stairs, but she shook her head, and told him the boy was asleep, so he sat down himself, going loose, hopeless, in the chair.

What the hell does it, he said, what starts it off?

But she shrugged, and he saw she had the knitting, and watched the needles begin, easily, moving in and out.

What a night, he said. What a goddamn miserable night.

It seemed nothing, and he grew restless, watching her, intent, and could say nothing, to break it. Getting up again, he asked her if she were tired, and so she put down the knitting, to follow him, blowing out the candle beside her,

while he took the other from the table to carry up with
them. But there was light enough, from outside, and so he
blew it out, to leave it again on the table.

Upstairs, he felt the room deeper, or open, the light
making a wideness, and breaking against the sides, pushing,
to make a space. He could not know that she saw it, but
hoped, and undressing, quietly, laid his clothes on the
chair, and got into the bed. He looked back to see she had
finished, and then felt her slide in against him, to sink back,
on the bed, then turn.

A place, she said, but didn't, and put her hands on him,
again gently, and he put his arms around her, still hoping.
The room was very light, and the whiteness now altogether
actual, seeming even a drift, of some wave, in, to make the
room a space, of an intention, or where one might come to
live.

Waiting, he went back against the pillow, easily, but
somewhere he heard the scream, behind him, and asked if
she would want him to go quietly, and being more, he
thought, that I can do something, perhaps which she might
wish me to. But she got up, and went into the other bedroom, opening the door then, so that he heard the sounds
very close to him, a pain there, and continuing. Quiet again,
she came back, but again it started, the boy calling, and she
went back.

All right, he called, asking, and she answered, soon, and
he lay back, tired, and a little lost. The moon seemed to
sink, a crest reached and lost, and he watched it, catching
the edge against the window, to try to hold it, but felt it
pass.

She came in, standing at the door, and waited to see if

the boy would now sleep, but he didn't, calling to her, and she went back.

What's the matter, he said, but she didn't hear. What's the matter, and she answered, again, soon, and he fell back again, to wait there, the night going deep, and on, he said, it must be late.

Then she got into the bed, and lay down, coming to him, then, but nothing, he thought, and heard it, the cry, and got up himself to run to the door, pulling at it, and yelled, what, seeing the boy sitting straight in the bed, staring, and crying, screaming, the sound driving in on him as he came.

What, he yelled, what, what, what, and got hold of the boy, by one arm, dragging him clear of the blanket, then bringing his own hand back, hard, to slap him, the head jerking back, and down. But useless, the screaming now louder, and he felt it useless, picking the boy up, to cradle him, holding him, and walking beside the bed's length, the moon still against them, a light, a light, he said, and went back to the other room to find her waiting with the candle.

Jardou

⁞ Jardou

*. . . und leise tönen im Rohr die dunkeln
Flöten des Herbstes . . .* —TRAKL

Clearing, the wind left, and the sky was very light, and walking along behind them, he sang, but softly, saying, you want to pick all the olives, but I will pick them all. And sang, again, feeling very good, the sky now altogether clear, and from behind the high house in front of them a single white light climbing down and falling all over them in one heap.

But she was in a hurry, and had the boy's hand in her own, to hold it, pulling, as they went on. We are late, she said, and looking back, found him still there behind them, and waited until he had come up to them, to take his hand too. Opening the gate, he went in and they went in after him.

I love you, he said, and stopped to shout, hello, and heard it echo around the building to be answered from the field, another shout, and they started, calling, the boy running in front of them.

He had expected some diligence, to put it that way, or some aspect of determination. But he now saw them almost finished, the mother by the furthest tree, reaching up and pulling off the olives. There was no hurry, he thought, and saw the trees were very old, the branches filled with the fine leaves, fluted, and still wet from the rain. He waved again, to the husband by himself, in the wet grass, and listening, heard the first sounds of their speech not understood, but it was, she said, *le jardin des olives.*

He listened, then went to the mother saying, hello, again, not caring that she would not know it. I love you, he said, but to the other, coming up now to join them, and she made a face back, laughing, the woman standing still nervous, her skirt held out to catch the olives which he began to toss down. Straining, he raked them clear, then dropped them to her, not looking, and saw the olives above him he could not quite reach.

Those, he said, and pointed at them, and his wife explained, the speech wavering, breathy, and she said, he thought, even things he could not understand. Bringing the chair, they both held it firm, and he got up on it, quite safe. Stretching, he picked more, leaning back to get them, and found himself among the higher branches. He picked what were left to give them to the woman, and shook the branches. Getting down, he looked at her, then felt the chair give and put out his hand and touched her, quickly, then stood on the ground.

Once there, they all sat down, and he lay back against the tree's trunk not caring about the wet. The father still sat past them, over to the side, and watched the children. They did not think to bother him at first, then called, and getting up, he came to sit with them.

They grew quite content, under the tree, the father

stretched out by the women, an old hat pulled down to the back of his head, nearly reaching the ears. His hair fell very straight beyond it, curling slightly at the neck.

But he was not, even so, unformidable. There was a very precise weight present. The younger man might not have budged it, he thought, but thought then of the woman, and looking, saw her dress almost worn out, and pulled tight about the shoulders.

I love you, he said, and echoed it in invariable silences saying, each time, I love you, but never feeling very much.

Shall we begin again, his wife said, and translated it, to them, so that they both stood up, waiting, but the father was not very interested.

You are not concerned, he said, but could not think of the right words, and his wife repeated it, to the man, smiling, and he shrugged in answer.

I had thought to pick olives, he said then, to his wife, and grew angry. This doesn't seem very close?

And laughed. One didn't care. And got the chair and brought it to another tree, placing it under the high branches, and then climbed up on it, to stand there. Following, both women took hold, so that he might have been their own, held there, in some attitude of attention.

Still the children ran by them, shouting, and played, very happy, the boy tagging after them to join in. Above them all, he looked down, thinking to pronounce any spell, perhaps, saying that it could be that way, but they waited, and he went back to picking.

He gave it, now, all care, parting the leaves with his fingers, and trying to find all those which might be left. It was difficult because the colors were too similar, and hiding in all shadows, it seemed there might be one more. But, below him, they pointed, and following their hands he saw the olives, and picked them, dropping them down.

All done, he said, but asked, and looking down, saw them pointing, and he reached out, to get it, then tossed it down to them.

Are you done, she said, and he got down off the chair, falling down beside them, then took the bag from the woman, smiling, to look at it.

Back of them, the father came back, and stood in a tangle of brush, and lifted a camera, holding it steady, to point, the hands very quiet. But the children would not hold still, and all crammed together until the father shouted at them, something, and they stopped and grouped themselves nicely, the grass brushing against their legs. He took the picture, then bent to wind the film, and went off to the house to leave them, there, by the trees.

Let go, the children would have run off but the mother held them, pulling down the youngest to sit on her lap, and he saw the cloth pull tight, watching, and called to his own boy to come.

Sitting him on his knee, he stroked the hair, the boy chafing, but held quiet there and let him do it. He would have spoken, but couldn't, and looking to his wife, wanted to push, then, at her, to explain, but did not know what he wished explained.

The woman watched, even so, intently, and smiling, he thought, or perhaps she smiled. Behind her, the other children stood all looking at him, and he wished to say something, but knew no words to.

She spoke to his wife, and listening, he heard them wander into sounds so very distant he could think of nothing they might mean, and said, stop it, and hearing him, his wife stopped, to smile, and getting up, he pointed again to the trees.

Some left, he said, but the women still sat and looked after him, and would not come. Behind him, their voices grew alien, and broke too far away to make him listen, so that he walked to the field's edge and turned to see no one but the children, still running among the trees. He watched, then brought them to him, calling, then sent them up into the trees for no reason, and they brushed past him, climbing up into the branches.

Waving, he tossed up twigs, and old bark, and looked for more in the trampled grass, then threw what he found up to see it fall, past the children, to the ground. One, now above him, sang, and he looked up to see her there, braced tight against the crotch of the limbs, and white along the ankles, and up the legs, to the skirt, and waved to her, crying out.

But she said, come, and turning, he saw them there now behind him, and nodding, he took the bag they had given her, and put it into his pocket.

The Boat

The
Boat

No one was moving but for William, and they paid him little attention. He came, now, down through the trees, and behind them, very carefully, to a huge rock that overlooked the water. The boat was too far out to see who was in it, but the sails looked beautiful, tight out and driving the boat through the water in a series of chopped lunges. He climbed up on the rock, took a stick he found there, and leaning out, dabbled it in the water. He wrote his own name three times, then his wife's, then those of their three children.

Way off up the field Mrs. Peter had talked of the weather, and she repeated herself, endlessly. The heat came, the sun rising very high and white in the sky, and beyond the field the trees in the orchard looked wilted and dull. She cried. Her face grew very tiny and alone, and with a sense of relief the other man, her friend, bent over quietly with a white handkerchief and dabbed at her eyes. He implored her to have reason, the conversation had been so tiring, and if they were to be together, ultimately, they must have the necessary courage. But she cried again, until her face was wet, and he held the handkerchief on her cheeks, rubbing them, hopelessly involved to be sure, but some small part of him seemed heroic and manly, and that was the part she looked to.

William, on the rock, knew nothing much more than the heat, and if the sun got any higher, he said, he would lose his mind entirely. The trees rustled slightly, the wind went past them with a murmur, but it was a hot wind, and William crawled down lower on the rock to wet his face in the water. And feeling it cool, he quickly took off his clothes and left them there, and jumped in.

All this the children were aware of, and in the boat they prepared to attack him, not sullenly, but as quickly as he had thought to go into the water like that, they as well saw him and wanted to surprise him by bearing down on him with the boat. They tacked, and the boat shuddered. For a minute the smallest boy's legs were covered with the foam, and he shouted to them all to look. But coming off, the boat righted itself, and again they watched William who swam beyond them.

Hence, in a vague way, it was all, Mrs. Peter said, a question of the heat. William could not hear her, he would not have heard her in any circumstances, but to her friend, recovered, the comment was apt and sensible. Weather as an inexhaustible subject, or he answered her, that this as well they would have to consider, and above all its effects on William's nerves. The right time would be precisely the time when, at an impasse with everything, and with, particularly, the heat, he should no longer give much of a damn about anything, and if he did treasure her, or anything, even so would give it all up quietly enough.

Supposition, she said, was not accurate. The wind blew. But to be in love was to be something, and if heat were elemental, they were likewise of nature's force.

It was a ridiculous time for anything. She couldn't really say that she loved him, and had to think quickly, which one. Her friend looked at her, her eyes were a little red but the face was not for him. He took her hand, because he wanted something, and she let the pressure come, then relax, and squeezed back a little and smiling, wondered again what would become of them.

William was not the question, she knew, or at least she thought it, and then kissed the other man, in almost trite fashion, saying it is very like it always is. And, do I now think what I think because I think other people have thought it. For this there was no reply, the kiss being remote, and very near insult. The speech anyhow a question, which the friend wanted to answer, but could not. He dressed in a loose shirt, worn outside of his pants, and with a check-like design. The pants were brown, something like khaki. He had black hair, and a small clipped beard on the end of his chin. To be romantic was to be insular in one's concern for others, and in love he acted as though he were looking in a mirror.

Against all that, viciously, the boat went on and in it the children hung one to the rudder, and one to the jib lines, while the third kept hold of the rope for the boom, and sighted William for the one sitting behind him. They were almost there. William's head showed itself a little off to the right, and with a sudden push, the rudder went over, and they were on top of him.

At that moment he saw them, and why he hadn't before, or heard them, he had no time to think of, but dove, the boat's bottom hitting his head. He went down and down, and in spite of it, thought of them all up there, on the surface. The boat had gone over, the water again grew light, and from his mouth a very thin line of little bubbles. Time passed, the weeds shone blue and green in the depth, the mud felt cool and close on his body. Then he gave a push with his feet and felt them sink in, then lift, and then he swam, up, and broke the water with a kind of gasped cry.

They were on the shore, and called out to him, and he answered by a wave of his hand and swam to them, slowly, feeling his head ache but had no resentment. The three children were there, the boat was now anchored and the sails rolled up, and tied. The rudder had been taken off, and lay across the back of the boat, drying. At the top of the mast a small red flag flapped in the breeze and the boat lifted and dropped in the ground-swell.

It was very lovely, he thought, but even more, this immediate solicitation, and pulling himself out of the water, he let himself fall into their hands, and be carried all the long distance to the house, as the friend took the bulk of the load by holding him under the arm-pits, gently, and lifting him very carefully so as not to joggle his head. He swore at the children, and they came behind him, somewhat afraid. He made no conditions, the sound of his own voice was ugly, or seemed ugly, to him. When he had been lowered to the sofa, he wanted to cry, and let them see it. But their faces were too far away, and he found himself asleep.

He dreamt of three tigers, in a forest. Their bodies were striped as he had expected. Their faces were long, with, on each one, a red tongue lolling out over white teeth. He gave a banana to each one of them. They ate the bananas, and put the skins to one side, whereupon he grew frightened, shifted his position, and began to snore.

Mrs. Peter continued with the business in hand, and she had no doubt that it was, despite the difficulties, an act that could be transacted as elaborately and as completely as the buying of potatoes. In the garden, she drew up a chair, close to the friend whom the matter of the boat had frightened. He felt himself now an outsider, or, more simply, unable to recover his own place with quite the same manipulation. To quiet him, she took off her sun-hat and began to fan herself, then fanned him, so that the moving air lifted the collar of his shirt, which he had left unbuttoned to the middle of his chest, and blew it against his beard.

Now, she said, that there is quiet, now we can settle all of this. He raised himself to listen, and to say what he himself would have to. She said, do you love me. To that, certainly, he replied, yes. They kissed.

But, she said, being married and all, does it matter to you that another man has had my love. And that was not a fair question. The woman who loves is beyond it, she does not see anything more than what she does have, just there and then, in front of her nose. He said, if it does not matter to you, it does not matter to me.

It was enough, and might have been for anyone else, but not for her. She wanted to go away, a long voyage, or anything to get away from him, and from both of them. Well, she said, I love you, but you don't love me. For my own part I think we are not so much in love as I had thought, but, seeing that we have no reason to hurry, take a walk to the beach, and in an hour I will come and join you.

Once he was gone, she went back into the house to look at William. He lay with an arm down over the edge of the

sofa, and she could see the place where the boat had hit
him. The bruise began at the edge of his hair, back of his
ear, then went into the hair itself. It all looked swollen and
painful. But she was not sure that she loved him.

If she whistled, or cried out, one of the two might come.
Otherwise, she then thought, I have three children. Who
would have killed their father this morning, and not even
meant to do it.

So it was impossible not to think about life, or the sense
of the kind of life she herself might find possible. The room
came in, a picture of her own father, or someone, hung at
an odd angle over the cold fireplace. There was no fire and
yet she screamed. But did not scream. In the emptiness she
saw William coming toward her, carrying an oar. He was
about to found a city.

As an alternative she left the room, and went out again
into the garden. The remains of their lunch were still there,
and, over the plates, she saw a swarm of flies. Looking past
them, she saw a briefcase, on the seat of a chair, with gold
initials just over the lock. She went over and picked it up,
and tried to open it, but could not, and threw it back in the
chair in anger. It was the life of a dead man, not to have
kindness, and openness, in each person met or dealt with.
To have secrets was finally to have desires, and if she could
not satisfy them, to keep them like that was dishonest. She
picked up the briefcase again and threw it into a bed of
yellow flowers. What she gave was open, and all air, she
thought. But for them it was the careful locking up of each
particular, because they thought they were men.

The children used another way of things, and taking in
the friend, now they played with him, and soon he was
exhausted, panting after them, foolishly, up and down the

beach. He had taken off his shirt, but they ran too fast, and if he caught one, another suddenly pelted him with a handful of sand, and, in trying to see which had done it, he lost hold of the one he had had, and found his eyes full of sand and tears.

He wanted her to come very badly, he saw their future life together floating over his head, and, as the wind might take it, blown away from him. He indulged in this metaphor, and was like a man lost in himself completely. If he wanted her, then, he thought, it must be that they leave together right away. To have the children, he said, and a stone hit him, and a small spot of blood appeared on the inner side of his ankle.

Mrs. Peter watched all this, and again was powerless. But, coming down, she told the children to stop, and from their own audacity, which they felt they had perhaps taken too far, they stopped, and ran down the beach and out of sight. Then she said, love me, very simply. And, as she asked it, he brushed off his pants, and came to her, and then led her back to the field, where they lay down. I want you to be for me, she said, but she hated him. As his hands touched her, she felt cold finally, and thanked him for that.

The Gold Diggers

The Gold Diggers

West of the mountains, the land rides out on a flat and open plain and continues for more miles than any one man ever knows of. The light is high, it comes from the farthest point of the sun. If you put a man here, already you find him lonely. If you put two, then what happens is not so much what either one man decides on, but what happens to them no matter.

For both of these reasons they built the shed in the shadow of one tree, which was the only one. To the back they put another slight covering for the machine, that is, the machine which dug for the gold. Sometimes it covered an acre a day, and on others, meeting with less, over twice that area. Their car stood back of it all under a thin canvas. In one of the rooms of the shed there was another machine which gave them electricity, and it ran on the same gasoline which they had provided for the other, at the first, making a cache of fifty large drums of it, at the far end of the site. That much was all safe, and because it had been regulated at the beginning, it now went on without significant interruption.

Only this night one of the men sat by himself on a chair

leaning against the tree. He had pushed back with his feet, and the chair lifted, and rested against the tree's trunk. The car was gone, and had left two days before, making a dust cloud far out over the dry ground to the east, and at last leaving him there, as now, sitting on the chair and watching. He said he could drink, and did drink, and left a single bottle, empty, on the ground. It was unpleasant. He sang to himself, and his voice rose out into the air, and against the sun he sang one thing that he could remember, which he called a lament. But he knew this loneliness.

Toward seven or eight the car came back, and at first he saw the small cloud of dust, which might have been made by some incredible stray horse, although there were none. It came closer and closer, and as it did he felt himself aching, and beginning to cry a little not much caring. The car came finally into the yard, and slurred past his chair to stop back of the shed. For a few minutes the doors stayed shut, and from behind the dusty windshield he could see the other man watching him. He tried to smile, but the skin of his face felt too cracked, so that he called out, in protest, and let himself wait for the other man to answer.

Getting out of the car, the man spoke, and motioned him to come over. Now he could smile a little, and saw the packages in the back of the car, piled up as high as the window. Reaching in, he took an armful and followed after the other man into the shed. He watched while the other man put his load down, by the table, but not on it. Then he put his own down.

There was nothing to say but he looked at him, knowing the face so exactly he could see the eyes pushed back into the narrow and quiescent head. He tried to say something, of the sitting there, but the other began to talk now, and they sat down together, facing, while the other paused to open one of the boxes, taking out two small bars of chocolate, and ripped the papers off both, first the shiny and smooth label one, and then the silver under it. He listened.

At first there was only a sort of low and discontinuous obscenity, the phrases marking out a street of the city he could not remember. He knew it was late. There was a bar, open, on the corner. The other man went in and sat down there. There were women.

One of them came up to him. He saw her head nodding under a high light, and some of it fell off the hair, glancing down to the glass in his hands. She was smiling at him or trying to also, and her hand had come forward enough to find his own. Speaking to her, his mouth was like the substance of his whole body, and twisted itself to answer. The low phrases continued, marking again and again each act of the meeting.

In her room she went completely into him, against his own will tearing at him, so that he left her, he thought, unconscious. The obscenities were now actual, they surrounded him. He thought of each thing, and could not even say who he was, or whether this had happened to him, or had not. When he made supper, because the other man was too tired and hardly ate it, he went in a daze, and even the food which the other had brought was almost something he could not taste.

The next day the sun cleared early, and getting out the machine, he oiled it. It looked black, and squat, on the ground. It moved like a tractor, and was long and low. The earth broke under it, shovelled into the front opening, and then ground down and down and down into small, and sortable, fragments. In a hopper at the back the gold itself slowly collected, in a half pure state. To some extent a man could become rich, insofar as the nature of the place allowed him that, and let the gold come up without difficulty. Here they found it uncertain, and some days travelled mile after mile without much of anything.

Because of practice he rode it easily, and without concentration. Before him the land spread flat. The mark of the other days was on his right, and there the land looked chewed and broken. In front of him it was utterly smooth, showing only a trace of rock, here and there, as something too far under him to be important perhaps came up to declare itself. But the gold was there. To that extent it was a job he had chosen for himself, although he had not known then what it would be. But that sort of argument he had the same contempt for he would show against any alternative, to the chosen thing, and had not as yet needed it.

Riding high, he set the steering wheel against his knees, and held it loosely with his hands. He kept his eyes low, clear of the glare of light from the horizon. Under him the machine moved along, carrying him straight forward.

So it went on. He didn't forget anything, but lumped it, now, altogether. He thought the light killed the woman, or the idea of her. He didn't know whether his companion was lying. Perhaps he was. There was no way to prove it. The machine grated on rock, then lifted and slid off, to dig in again ahead of it, and continue. He never looked back because he thought he would not be able to bear it, like a cut on his hand when the blood came too fast. Now he rode it, or drove it, regardless.

Then he stopped. He got down from the seat, swinging clear of the treads with a push of one hand, and landed hard on the ground. For a moment he crouched there, leaning against the machine, and then looked around the back of it to the shed. But for the car again, there was nothing different. The tree was there. The shed stood over from it only a short distance, and the door was shut. He couldn't see anyone, and thinking to call, stopped himself, and got back up on the machine.

But it was a persistent thought. Somewhere in the screaming, still under him, the sound alone enough to kill out any other, even so there was something else. He would have driven a tractor the same way, and could see no difference possible. He made as straight a furrow as he could, and at the end, let it rear on the turn, to settle again to the run back. Forcing it only a little, he judged he could make it in an hour, and settled himself back to watching the shed reappear, at first a small and indeterminate blur, then larger, until at last he saw it almost clearly, and the tree again beside it.

When he came in, the other man started to talk to him. He told him more of the trip, with the car, and took each mile as it had come, the rabbits shying in front of the lights at night, then the flat emptiness of the day, until, at last, he saw the first towns coming up to him, and then the city. But it was not really possible to believe it. Together they knew everything, and nothing, because one false thing and none of it was true. He thought, he didn't even like the other man, and was with him because he needed him, but not in a way that he might. He poured out the water, carefully, and got the bottle the other had brought from the cupboard and put it on the table beside the plates. Drink, he said, damn you. You have all the fun.

You want to know a real woman, the other said, some

real fine thing. Because that's why I stay here at all. To
earn money.

He didn't answer him. He put the rest of the things on
the table, and pulled up his own chair to sit down. A real
woman, the other man said. One with real hair, and real
legs, and real eyes. Real, he said.

But the plates were clean, the food left, unavoidably,
dried, and hardened, on the tin. The other man got up and
pushing them all together, he picked them up and carried
them off to the bucket. He sat down beside it, and poured
some water into another tin, and sloshed it over the dishes.

There was nothing to say. He watched the other man's
hands, he saw them take the dishes, rubbing them. The
water poured over them, back to the tin, then repeated,
until the other man got up, and wiped them all with his
hand, shaking them, and put them beside the tin on a shelf
to dry. It was time to go.

Once again on the machine, the sun came down, clearing
his head, he thought. The noise came again. It started as
the motor started, then ground deeper into the final sound
of the machine moving, and the earth lifting into it. He
whistled, and high above the sound could hear the thin,
sighing noise. Now he rode the machine, letting it take him,
like a horse. Perhaps the gold rattled into the box. The
lumps were as big as his fist, he scooped them up, and let
them fall through his fingers. Somewhere the whole noise
was constant, and became a continuity through which he
rode the afternoon.

So he drove carefully. Now and again a ragged patch of
mesquite, or some bush, passed him, or else he struck it
head on, eating it up. Far ahead sometimes the sun glinted
on rock, and as he came up to it, he eased the machine,

then hit it. There was the lifting motion, and then they went on. Time after time the plain blurred, and to his eyes it was an ocean, or a place without any disturbance at all. The sun flattened it, it pressed hard in, and down, and forced the nature of the ground itself out.

Then, turning, he saw the woman, not really as even he knew, but there she was even so. He felt embarrassed by the noise, and the nature of the work he was doing. He wished the dust might be not so thick, or the roar so heavy he could not even speak to her. He had no hat that he could rightly raise for her, since the cap he did wear seemed impossible to him to lift. All of it was impossible, he saw her float for a moment, clear of the ground, then she was gone completely. He let the idea stay inside of him. He thought he would never speak of it. He let the roar come back, and drove ahead, sighting the shed, and watched the tree grow larger beside it.

But that night he spoke of it. It was night in the shed now. They ate. The other man got out the bottle and they drank, and he sat there listening to the other man talk again. There were other things to be said. The pictures came, faded, and came back. The woman was all alone. It was an echo coming again and again, back, and in the words of the other, with no intention, continuing until he spoke at last himself, telling all of it, of her being there, and then not there, and finally fell down himself, crying and crying, until the other pulled at him, to make him stop.

You should stop, the other man said. There's no good in that, you wait a minute.

He heard nothing but the sound of the other moving away from him, back to a corner of the room. He waited. His eyes were wet but he made no move to rub them. He

lay still forward on the table, keeping his head covered
with his hands. Behind him the sounds shifted to a rattling
of some paper, something unrolling, and then again he
heard the man walking across the room to him. The hand
pulled at his shoulder, lifting him, and light hit his face,
while the other said, look, pushing it at him, the odor incredible but certain, and again the light fell off the silk and
the hair into his eyes.

He went forward, grabbing at the cloth. The other man
fell down still holding it, and then sat, on the floor. He
kicked at him, and the other fell over completely and rolled
flat on the floor, then quiet. The room was quiet. He bent
over and picked up the table, and lifting it as high as he
could, he let go.

The Suitor

The
Suitor

Let them say 'tis grossly done, so it be
fairly done, no matter ...
—THE MERRY WIVES OF WINDSOR

Staggering back along what he took to be the path, he
thought, long roads are happy roads, and continued.
Somewhere inside the shape now looming beside him, like
they say, was also the woman he loved, or had taken himself
to, as she had apparently also taken him to. Not to mention
her mother, amiable woman, who at least allowed him bed-
space. There was a kind of gaiety about it all, and since the
party was over—it was about four in the morning—he felt
he might well be the last one so possessed.

Kate, he called, through the door, and fell through it
because the light stayed off, firmly off, and decidedly. But
where was she, in the dark? He listened for sounds of
breathing and heard, from somewhere in the blackness, a
sough, a kind of sighing wheeze, which hardly bore him
much confidence. So he waited, even held himself, quiet,
and said, again, Kate?

Finally it answered him, to wit, the dull black form on
the bed, now a little at least visible, as it raised itself on an

elbow almost, he thought, god bless her, like his own mother, last seen waving to him across or obscured by the tailgate of a truck. But he would never run away from home again. What home he had, could have, there he stayed, forever.

But it was a short night. He heard them talking in the kitchen, through the open doors, of the living-room, and looked out from under the sheets. There was a large painting on the wall opposite him. The voices said, first we will take knives and cut little bits out of his knees, eyes, and toes, and then we will cover him all over with flour, and lard, and push him into this nice big oven, for which we have ordered one ton of coal. She said, he heard it, the coal has come. Will you? He nodded, and she backed out of the room, closing the door behind her.

It was part of the system. To eat is to work, he worked. He got up, dressed quickly in the same clothes he had already, he found, been already, partially, dressed in. He had never taken them off. But once in the air, he took stock of his surroundings. The house across the street had certainly moved in the night. It crowded close to the fence which, he supposed, was the only thing holding it back. In one of the windows a face pressed hard against the glass, looking. He turned and saw, then, a large pile of coal which had been dumped close to a bulkhead which he briefly opened, and began to shovel.

How much later he was never to know there was a rustle at the screen-door also by the bulkhead, and he saw, dimly, someone motioning to him. Come in, she said. He came in. Sitting down, he took up the cup of black coffee gratefully. Thank you, he said. He drank it, gulping a little, an odd but definite constriction in his throat which even the half-cooked egg, eaten later, failed to dislodge. There was no toast because the bread had not yet been got. She said. She looked at him. He looked at her.

Once again he began, this time singing, he did not know why, but soon there was standing close to him a small boy of about ten years, listening. What would you like to hear, he thought. There was certainly enough to tell. Sometimes he thought even of writing it all down, and of then putting it into a bottle, and of then throwing it out the window. Somehow it might arrive on a beach.

Otherwise there was not very much to hope for. The coal was shovelled, all of it, but then there was the bread to be got. He trotted down the road, down the hill, wondering if his buttocks joggled too preposterously. Love had no objections at least. But it also occurred to him, why should it. There were compensations. In the store he asked for one loaf Italian bread, and they gave it to him. Whereupon he handed them the folded dollar, and they returned him change.

This he gave back to them, not to them, but to the two women now in front of him. The bread he put on the table. There was never a clear demarcation between times. Sometimes, idiotically enough, he thought he was sitting in a chair. But if this were so, and if he had taken the bath sometime ago, being obviously dirty, why now should he be objected to? The water dripped from a crack in the ceiling over his head. The mother looked at him, greying hair, grey hair, he thought. She said, oh, you must have sloshed, in your bath. Blackly, he felt himself gripping the arms of the chair but it was an iron slung chair, or something. He sat precariously enough.

No, I did not, he said. How could he prove such a thing?

Next time they would certainly think themselves entitled to watch. He sat on the toilet, gripping, dully, the fact that in order to flush it one must bend over, somehow, and turn the little tap handle underneath the seat so that the water could then fill the bowl. And hence, away! There had been that scene. Someone had wanted to brush her teeth. Take me away, he thought. He picked up a magazine and tried to remember how to read.

On page five she asked him if he were thirsty. It was five o'clock? After five o'clock one could drink, seriously. Up till then, beer and wine. She handed him the glass. On the glass, in adhesive tape, was the large, slightly frayed initial, *R.* For rest, he thought. Do you have my glass, the other said, the mother. Is your name ratface? How could he say it? It was too true. She took the glass, smiling, and another was handed to him. Ratface, he thought, ratface, ratface, ratface. I hate you, ratface. He thought.

But there was a scratching at the door, then another face. The face, he saw, of old Bill Bunch, lately hailed, at least frequently, by both mother and daughter as that lovely and impossible man. He was their next door neighbour, so that was helpful. Gossip had it that he could do very little, if anything. He fumbled, he tripped, one time when his son was sick (the ten year old of earlier acquaintance) and then his wife likewise, in the care of the former, and the man, Bill, sent to a hotel in the city to keep him out of the way or under cover, depending on the inference, anyhow he returned home, to help, and tripped walking up the steps and sprained both ankles. No one is safe, he thought. Bill smiled.

Fumbling, Bill took his drink, then faded back to the

porch not yet in need of paint, and sat there, with all the security of a man who is an alcoholic and knows it. They would never let him forget it. Why he came here at all, who could say? The mother went after him.

So they were alone, there was a pause, then she turned on the phonograph. He winced. There was a scratching not unlike Bill's, then music, a man singing, screaming rather, a song. The singer was also interesting, like everything else. He was an ex-professor. He had lost his job at any rate. Perhaps to buy the record at all was legitimate charity. It was horrible.

Holding on to the glass, he looked at her. She sang to him, the same song. Along with the record. Let me take you away from all this, he said. It was a reasonable hope. He had shown her his letters. One possible employer wrote, *I should like very much to meet you if you are ever up this way.* Many men have started with less. Take him as anything they could get. That is, they had him. Sweep floors. Putty windows. Paint porches. Shovel coal. But the ton would last longer than that. He hoped. He looked at her. She looked at him.

Coming back in, the mother sat down again. Bill had been dismissed. Through the door, still swinging, he caught sight of an empty glass. How sad to be remembered! No one will do that for me, he thought. Cold wind, icy ground, put no wreathes, down here. Keep talking.

But the subjects were limited, at least now they were. They had heard most of his own stories, he had heard all of theirs. It was a deadlock. Ten more minutes, and they would all be dead. Or at least might be, except to keep drinking, also, and talk, the voices again becoming even last

night's. So that to live was a very definite retrogression.
Tomorrow will be yesterday, when you see the whites of
their eyes, don't shoot.

A gun anyhow was what he wanted. A cool deliberate
aim, to lift it, to hold it, pressed close against his shoulder.
Here they come, he said. Pam, pam! You're stoned, George,
said mother. Ok, he said, I give up.

The Musicians

The
Musicians

He walked out with her behind him. At least she stood there, still, hidden from the doorway but to the side, listening, as he went past her, and out into the hall. She was saying, he's there, although the hall was empty. If there was someone there, then he was not there now. He stopped to say, you see, and continued, no one. There is no one here at all. But she closed the door, hard, and left him standing, facing to the stairs.

So at this moment he saw the other man, like, as he thought, that now of course there he would be, to be alone with him. It was where he hadn't looked, above him, the stairs going up obliquely, to the roof, and now the man came down them and said, good morning. He answered, good morning, John. The sun was bright, what was it, eight or nine. One could go out, on the street, walk two blocks, go into some place, sit down, buy perhaps coffee, black perhaps, and a roll or whatnot, and that would be that and nothing more. But he had something else to do. Look, he said, John, come with me, that is, can't we get out of here? He thought, I knew you in school, one time I slept on top of you, with a mattress between us, which is love of a sort,

is it not. His eyes filled, with tears. We're friends still, he
said. You don't kill all that that easily? But caught himself,
because how easy was it, to do it, anything, anytime, even
with anyone.

Behind him the man walked down the stairs very quietly,
his face down so that it could not be seen. This was simply
protective. They went out, at the bottom of the stairs, the
one in front of the other, expecting, at least the one in front
did, to be there mowed down, a sudden abrupt barrage of
machine-gun fire, cutting them precisely in half. The sun
dropped past them, to the flat concrete of the courtyard.
And tonight you will do the same thing, he thought, you.
Getting up makes no difference whatsoever. To anyone. He
walked across the courtyard and opened the door into the
other half of the building. The hall was yellow, an ochre.
They went along it, past the boxes for mail, and out into
the street.

Here it was somewhat simpler. Forced, if there were anything, to happen, then a sidestep, or a push, could bring
him past it, hidden against a doorway, or jammed into
strangers who might, he thought, help him. This was a
story of violence and murder. Three found dead, in a bed.
Which, bitterly, the bed itself prevented, being not big
enough. What would you like to eat, he said, and added,
John, have you eaten? The man came up, then, and walked
beside him. You know, he said, it wasn't easy. The man
walked, beside him. How could it be easy, he said. Words
poured into him, from everywhere. How, he said. Look,
you know me.

As they went past the door of a cafe, the man made a
sign, to go in, but would not go in himself. So he went in,
and bought coffee, to go out, then some rolls, which he also

thought indicated, and went out when he had them but he
saw nothing of the man, and remembered he was to walk
back, and up to the man's room, and they would eat, then.

He used this time to reconnoitre, which phrase he got, or
had got, from the account of a British, he remembered, spy
in Germany during the first World War. The man wrote, at
length, of how he had managed to break over the line,
between the two armies, and then by virtue of a straight
face, hardly more, and a knowledge of the language, which
was also given, he worked his way up and up, till at last he
was actually in the group of the German Command itself.
Work and work, keep at it, you too will be on top. An
irony. But nonetheless where he both had been, he thought,
and well might land again, helpless as he was to stand
against it.

But, opening the door, he saw this plan was useless. The
room in front of him scattered, fell into, many patterns.
There was a picture of a long low car, an old one, tacked on
the wall over a table. There were records, and beyond
them, a small black phonograph. Simply enough, this was
his friend. Well, he said, do you want proof? Which photograph shall I show you. Or, simply, the first, of a man,
standing by himself in a street, somewhere in Mexico City.
Or rather he walked along the street and because he did, or
John did, his picture was taken, a small card given him,
which he, John, must have remembered later, and he got
the picture and he, John, sent it home. A fact. He had seen
it certainly. He had admired it. How nice to live in Mexico!
There was another, as well, a man sitting at a table, in a
long low room, a round one, which seemed unusual. On the
table there were some plates left over from eating. A girl, a
pretty girl, sat past him and had her head bowed. The

picture was large, the whole feel of it seemed to mean that
someone had both cared to take it, and, having taken it,
cared also to print it like this. So that it could be something
not just a cheap snapshot, however much that is all right
too, but something also better, more durable, simply more
careful.

Are you hungry, he said. He put the food and the coffee
on the table, and then, unwrapping it, offered it to his
friend. Where shall I begin, he said. Perhaps I could tell
you a story, too? Let's put it, two men, ourselves, we live in
a long black house, like that one. He pointed to the car, on
the wall. Every morning at ten o'clock sharp we take it out
of the place, wherever we keep it, and we drive it, like hell,
up and down, up and down. We love it. We think there is
nothing either greater or any damn thing else. By God, we
enjoy ourselves. Then one day, because some idiot turns
left on a street where there is a huge, huge sign saying, do
not turn left, that's it, the end of us. The goddamn car so
smashed, broken, disintegrated, that really we have nothing
at all left. So we go out and so on, maybe to a hospital,
where a beautiful nurse in a long black uniform, I think,
sews us up, good as new, and then we get another car.

Can't we get another car, he said. Can't we do it? The
man drank the coffee, lifting the cardboard cup very carefully. Are you listening. John, he said. Can't you hear a
goddamn thing I am telling you? But then he sat back, and
also drank his own coffee, slowly. Look, he said, John.
There are other ways than this to tell it? He stopped. Are
you listening to me? The man smiled, and got up, and
turning on the phonograph, put on a record, and sat down.

At that the room became still, though there was the music, a low quiet thing, perhaps a trumpet, he thought, if I

can still remember. You play the piano, don't you, he said. He thought. A face, John's face, hair cut short, clipped. A man's funny odd hands, on a piano, that is, on the keys of a piano. Even, if it mattered, Boston, Mass. The end.

Play it for me, he said, *me*. He stopped. Did you ever hear the one about there must have been three of them, people? He said, there were three people, a man, a man, a woman. God knows where they lived, a house? Ok. Not long and black this time, this one is snow-white, has clapboards like in the movies, roses, the works. Every morning not only the milkman comes, he brings two dozen milks, the greatest, but also, mind you, at least the plumber, the mailman, the electrician, the hairdresser, the modista, the maestro who fixes the walls when they fall down on your head because you will pound on them. Ok, he said. What can I do more than that?

The man sat, watching. Behind them both, and through the window, there was the upper side of the building opposite, breaking off into a line of others, the roofs of them, even more broken. Looking, he caught sight of a small crouched figure, on the roof next to their own, above their heads, and it was her, sitting there, with some kind of pyjamas on, with a bathrobe over them, to cover her.

Look, he said. See this. The man got up and went over to the window, then sat down again.

By god, he said. You know, John, I haven't really tried and let me do that at least. He stopped again and coughed, and added, what the hell do you like to drink, at which the man bent over and pulled a bottle of sherry out from underneath the bed, uncorked it, and handed it to him. He swallowed, quickly, and handed it back.

It's never easy, he said, never. What should I say, that I

was walking down the street? When suddenly, and from out of nowhere, comes a truck and hits me? That's love, John. Nothing more, nothing less. You had a mother?

The man said, don't talk about my mother, saying it carefully, so that he stopped, again, to listen to him. Because he did not know John's mother, but wanted to, not for maudlin reasons, but there it was, something unknown, and a pleasure. Why don't we go to Mexico, he said. He watched the man carefully. There's a bus, he said, it's not impossible?

Or work, he said. Look, I would like to work, I would like to do something outside. He made a movement of his hands, and there it was, perhaps a big hole in the ground, in which others sweated, but never himself. I would like to get out of this.

John, he said, for the last time, look. Nothing is easy. Because, he said, three things matter. That one eat, that one sleep, that one make it. Three finite actions, which can, I think, be accomplished?

The man got up, coming toward him, saying, to go, as he knew, and behind them, also she moved, on the roof, and seeing that, then it was ugly, unsimplified. Don't cry, he said. That doesn't help.

The Dress

The
Dress

$\mathcal{M}$uch was simple about Mary and Peter, and to describe them quickly, it was first of all two people, in a house into which not many others came. And three children, pushed into corners, and a friend or two who came to call. After ten years or so of living together, there were no very actual mementos, or none that either felt much disposition to recognise. There were no flags, and in fact few signs of even time except for the children, and a scar which traversed Mary from belly-button to bottom. Which both had *done*, but also for which Peter was in some sense guilty. Not her.

But, passing that, walking into the room, at this instant, saying something, Peter wanted one action, definite, to place them all in that place where time shall have no dominion. Louise, Mary's *present* friend, was a tall woman, dangling happy jiggly things hung from both ears with such weight that he was worried her ears might tear loose. The pain of speaking was in this way increased.

But. Now—for once he shook free of it, taking with him both Louise. And Mary. And through a small opening in the floor, pulled them down, into where *he* lived. Saying nothing, because there was nothing to say, *now* he led them through a tiny passage, obliging Louise in particular to crawl on all embarrassed fours, like the tiny and comfortable being she was. He snapped a whip. He turned on a light, and, in an instant, the cavern was flooded with a warm rich yellow searching glow. Peering into the two faces looking up at him, he saw, first, dismay. Then, laughter. And then, dismay. So back up they went, into the room, and sat there.

Mary's dress, half-finished, lay on the table, and this is what the two women had been talking about, planning, deciding, when he had, first, come in. It was a question as to whether this material, as an added border, and so, design, would be the best, the most interesting, or, on the other hand, that. Two materials lay beside the half-finished dress, in long narrow strips, and on one there was a quiet, rich, oblique design of some warm grey and blue and red. And on the other, a more excited, flaring, intense design of green, yellow and blue. Louise asked him what he thought would look best, and Mary, by her listening, also was curious to know. So he thought, *under* the dress will be, of course, Mary. So what is Mary like? Yet that necessitated returning to *under* the floor, so down they all went again, the women this time less hesitant, as he drew them on, and down, and also more curious to explore, should he let them, this sudden, exciting inclination.

He let them explore, and as the yellow light reached all corners of the underfloor cavern, the two women went, hand in hand, to one after another of the sights which were there. As, for example, the stalactites and the stalagmites. Which had been formed by the dripping, and which hung, like icicles, from the roof of the cavern, or else rose like spikes, from the floor of the cavern. The dripping itself was from a fissure, a cleft or split. But also, a narrow opening in an *organ,* as was now the case. A cleavage. Findo. To *cleave.* Peter had accomplished this by a daily *expenditure,* and these objects, precariously enough arrived at and/or created, were important to him.

The women moved incautiously, because these things were not what he had *done,* not, that is, what they had done for him. Mary did many things for him, as she now did, certainly, in the present place—by moving there at all —and by looking, touching, exploring. Louise, striking one of the pendular accumulations with the hard heel of her hand, said, listen! And from the hanging, or rather the hanging up spike-like accumulation, came notes, with each blow, like those of Big Ben chiming the hour, in London. Peter brusquely silenced her, and it was then that both women reminded him of their reason for coming to the cavern, at all.

So again they sat in the room, with the dress material across Mary's knees, while she bent over it, as if to catch, now, in some pattern of the varied cloth, an instance of her own person. Finally, in short, this was to be her own *person,* or at least was, from, roughly, the knees to the neck, with arms and varied other areas left clear. Under it of course would be her own body.

Louise interposed the *idea* of, in New Mexico, Indian women, with their many layered dresses, built out into a raging, piled, and then formed piece of clothing. This, with the hair pulled back, long, and left to hang down. Also, they had straight backs, fine clear features, a race altogether of clean dark women. Under this onslaught Mary buckled, adding for herself a host of other details, taken

from pictures of Mexican women, Italian women, and the
more known Spanish women. Peter himself saw his wife as
white, and had known her as such. He added to the material which she held, on her knees, the memory of other
materials, and, in particular, one thin worn black and
purple-spotted dress, for which he had a great fondness.
This dress, when she wore it, swelled into desirable propor-
tions, the breast forward, the waist drawn in, and for the
neck, low and round, of the dress, a leaving open of the
bones, which formed the height of the body, wide, then
certain, down, into the complexity of the *flesh*.

It was the friend's *premise*, however, to make the wife
not a wife? This was where Peter himself was confused. To
take Louise, too, into the cavern—she was with Mary and
that allowed it. Louise, looking at him, now, was *older* than
he was. As, in some crowded neighborhood, this building
is older than that one, and, because it is, insists on itself as
in that way more rightly there. Under any dress the body is
this or that, older or younger, whiter or darker. Under the
floor he had the cavern to think about, but Louise could not
think *about* it. She was either there or not. Mary likewise.

Mary, the young wife, getting up, put the cloth on the
table where it had first been, and went out to see about
supper. In the room behind them Louise and Peter heard
her speak, then the maid answer, then Mary speaking,
again. Whether or not the children had always been in the
room, as they now were, looking at both Peter and Louise,
covetously, was not certain. Could he take *Louise* into the
cavern? Alone?

In the cavern Louise stood back from him, crouched under the warm yellow light, and hidden behind the multiplic-
ity of forms which crowded from all sides. He spoke, yet

the voice in finding her became too changed to be recognized. It was not his voice. Had he thought of her otherwise, he might well have *approached* her. But he did not. Soon other faces looked down, from that point at which they had entered the cavern, little faces looked down, three in number. This time Louise did not strike the coagulated, hardened and depending forms, with her hand. No tone, at all, broke the silence.

Yet the relief was in the *body*, both his, and hers, and also Mary's. Who was not present but was felt, among them, and each, Louise and himself, insisted on that knowledge. In the yellow light one group of stalactites and stalagmites appeared to be a castle. Another seemed a forest. Another, not far from where Louise continued to *creep*, back, on hands and knees, was a snow scene, and reared, up and down, in sinuous, fixed motion.

When Mary re-entered the room Louise spoke to her, but Peter was unable to. He remained in the cavern. But concern soon brought him out, and closely listening, he accepted the invitation of their words and re-addressed himself to the problem of material.

Was the dress to be final—is in effect how he addressed it. The *body* was not final, yet women, or rather his wife, she was final. Louise was not. In the cavern, revealed, or veiled? In that light it was Louise, entire, who was revealed. In the mind, or idea, of Peter.

Picking up the material again, Mary let it spread over her knees, and looked at Peter, and then, at Louise. The concern was whether or not the dress was to be her own person, or Louise's? Or the Indian women. Or, in the cavern, all these forms were taken care of, redisposed, in, surely, a wide variety of *attitudes*. Peter wanted a dress, for Mary, that would not be Louise, at all. He wanted, desperately enough, to make the *body* present, all of it, by simply that clothing of Mary, which would not re-displace her, not again. Each time she left the room he thought she would never come back. He was left with Louise.

Left with Peter, Louise turned to Mary. It was Mary's suggestion that, in the cavern, they wear *no* clothes, because she was Peter's wife. But Louise wanted the dress. She arranged the dress, on Mary, and then chose the intenser, more flaring design of green, yellow and blue, from the two materials either one of which she might have added. To finish the dress. Peter laughed but felt dismayed, too. This was to be Mary's *own* person. Mary readjusted the half-done dress upon herself, and held the material, which Louise had chosen, against it. The dress, with the material, became her.

But the *cavern* was and *is* an underfloor hollow, with a *horizontal* entrance. And is made by the *subsiding,* or *giving inwards,* or *smashing in,* of *soil, walls,* etc. Cavern-dwellers are *prehistoric men* living in these huge or deep *hollows within solids*. Peter said.

The Book

The Book

He was bringing the book in a gesture of final hope, something he had found in a bookstore just after leaving her. *Oh bright and sunny day,* and words to an old English time and tune, measure of clear voice and air. She liked to sing, in a high clear voice, a little thick at times, chirruped, like a secure bird. The book was a paperback collection of English Aires and Folksongs, edited by authentic people she would be careful to see.

Down the street, walking heavily along, it was time to be not drunk but the afternoon was heavy and slow, he was drunk with beer and dirtiness. All over his body, sluggish sweaty clothing under the dusty sun, walking more than he was used to, the streets were hard and barren.

She had a number of songs she would sing. At one time it is possible that she might have been trained to sing professionally. It was a leftover hope in that sense, a little of an ability put to fond memory's sake and trust to it to reappear, always. They do not forget what they meant to do, but just don't do it. She sang not happily altogether, not wildly, certainly, nor loudly, sadly, strongly, longly. Just enough to be the memory, turn on the radio, the victrola, and listen. Concerts and early training were the strengths she had.

She had painted also. She had been trained in that in a large grey building along a dark avenue of the city. It was a timorous place, yet aggressive with age and authority of that kind. He once rented a room on that street. He had to go through the living-room of the owners to get to his own room, through theirs to the back. He moved his things in, sat on the bed for only a few minutes and then apologized and moved out. Had he apologized? The sins of walking are the sins of memory, and she was not in that at all.

He lit a cigarette and considered his direction. A drug-store lay on his left at some distance, a flat square with a few trees in a triangle beyond it, then across, a row of usual businesses along the same avenue.

She was there somewhere in that maze. At another crossing of a street, a hotel for women, Y.W.C.A., kindest of all refuges, heaps, of people, who must be secured, for a moment, against sex, age, and other identity.

Earlier, "I didn't expect you so quickly, I had just come down." He had called her, at the desk, a woman watching him in dull glasses, piled hair, but prim, and not friendly. Who came here? Ask for your wife, mother, sister, the girl friend, is she here? Like a morgue of women, that sex, all of them, beds and beds and beds of them. Think of the sound, snoring, wheezing, blowing, puffing, breathing, in beds in sleep.

"Not about that," he wanted to say. "Don't," she was saying, and she was crying. "I don't want to go through it all again. I can't tell you more. I don't know more. There isn't any more to tell."

Explain. I was raped on the boat, not raped but like that.

I lost a thousand dollars in a purse, on the train. I bought a lot of Italian blouses. I do what I want to, now.

What is the English song? Something like, *I want to go where the birds go.* Not quite, but that flavor of old softness, a deep blanket of cold clear warmth. Hush, they are singing, *down in old Bethlehem the lights are low.* No but carefully, you can't get it right all the time. The note goes up there, then, one, two, down it goes. Lightly. *They came upon,* not so common, it is, *a statue, weeping at grief.*

It was a brutal dullness that he felt, walking. Having intended to do it, he wanted to do it, and with the book in his hand, wet with the sweat of his hand, from walking, it was not new. It was a dirty old plan, with the walking. The old book worn with the intention of taking it to her. As though next week he had remembered a plan which he had thought of and done, accomplished, paid bill of something or other. No history in that, nothing solved, no answer because he was being overcome by the action of walking toward her, the time climbing up on him as though it were a weight he accumulated step by step.

Can't you sing, too? No, I don't feel easy doing it, I try to hard enough, try too, hard enough. No but I can't. Can't you? No.

Would he ever see her again in this life, he thought. This day perhaps, again. Talking at lunch with food he did not like, want, to eat, a failure in that so reminiscent of his meals with her, and for years to come quite the same. Oh he wouldn't change. That was the song.

He had meant everything he had ever done. Not to do many things, to do a few also.

"Oh where do the birds go when the summer's sun is through?"

No, but closer, a little closer, each time. The words go
along a line in movement with the song, the song is in that
way a song, of words. That tell what? Oh common things,
of women and men, lads and lasses, hay, corn fields, horses,
old roads, stones and crows, roses and one begins, "I remember, I remember, the house." Not so common but later,
earlier, into some practice of ear and voice he knew nothing
of. Say it slowly.

"Waley. Waley. Oh, love is bonny. A little whi(high)le
while it is new." That was the true one, the right one. Sing
it. It was in the book which he held in his hand. A docu-
mented pair who had done the selection assured her, would
assure her, they were all there.

Sing:

> *The street is the book is*
> *in the garden*
> *sitting on your knee*
> *my dear old England . . .*

Sing of her, that is the garden's insolence, that bent the
seat she sat in, broke the thorn to get a better hold, to stick
it in the face of winter's thorn, bleak wind and cutting frost,
aghast upon the frozen pane, the wind doth drive upon,
fast night, fast moon, stuck fast in ice today. English songs
are pretty little songs with a right, bright tune which fol-
loweth.

The book in his hand had a slight weight, but the heat of
the hand as pressed against it, holding it, was the bother of
it. He had no idea as to which street would most quickly
get him ·there. He wandered, a little drunk still, hence
walking head forward steadily. People he supposed to be

looking at him, or after, but he could not change his eyes. They went forward as his feet.

He listened slowly, closely, to all that she played him, on the phonograph. He had burnt out the fuses on two floors of the building in which they lived, fixing it better, more volume, more sound to it. The bump and grind of calypso, Charlie Parker. Listen to it. The song is, *oh where do the birds go, you don't see them any more now.* No but you can't hear it enough, so sweetly, so lightly. Hear it. Listen closely, then pick up the instrument and play it. Blow, this way, across, making the sound lift out of the long wood. Hold it firmly but do not over-press. A sound as in woods' hollow, from furtive shadow and water, the reeds and willows of the wood. Not to be learned in an instant. Listen, and again, listen. He sang with a sharp croak, oh shut the door behind you. She was always not shutting the bathroom door.

In a maze of people, streets, then brought to doors, one after another of them, or parks like deserted, contaminated areas, as if cut off, out, of the activity, as if to be rebuilt as parks one day, woods, hollows, water. A pipe dripped water into a stone basin. He wet his hands and then wiped them on his pants. He sat down to think of his direction.

"Not ever again," she said. No but one last time, say. This was outside the call of duty. One last look, book, like not forever, but one last time, Hey it's you! By god, it's you. I never expected to find you here like this. Oh say, what a happy day, you came my way, and that was a song. Sing it.

He got up no longer knowing where he was. He asked the man passing where it was, and got a vague answer. The drunk with the book. Look, the drunk's got a book. A new book. They wouldn't answer him but went past quickly, smiling, frowning. Perhaps he would try to sell the book to them.

He wasn't that drunk. He was heartbroken. He was hot, tired with walking, wanted to drink beer, wanted friends, a home, wife and friends and beer. He sang a song for that sound. He kept on walking but it wasn't fair any more.

You're not listening. Yes but he couldn't get the words. Like this, and one, and two, like this, and, there, you hear it, now, and one, and two. *The boy stood in the burning bush. His hair was all on fire. He thought that he would burn to death. And very soon expire.* Yes but not, like this. Song it is, wrong it is. He kept walking because the plan had been made, no longer to be thought of as anything else. Get the book to her. Get the goddamn book to her. Show her what you can do. The book with the songs.